NOT QUITE
A PRINCESS

THE BOSTON HEIRESSES BOOK 4

AVA ROSE

CONTENTS

Chapter 1   1
Chapter 2   12
Chapter 3   21
Chapter 4   32
Chapter 5   39
Chapter 6   47
Chapter 7   62
Chapter 8   74
Chapter 9   87
Chapter 10   100
Chapter 11   109
Chapter 12   126
Chapter 13   139
Chapter 14   147
Chapter 15   157
Chapter 16   168
Chapter 17   181

Also by Ava Rose   197
About the Author   199

CHAPTER ONE

BOSTON ATHLETICS CLUB FOR WOMEN

November 20, 1895

"This is not how I envisioned my day would go." Princess Mary Armstrong-Leeds nocked her bow and drew, her gaze intent on the target as she slowed her breathing.

"How did you envision it? Out at the modiste with your Mama?" The sound of Lillian shuffling her feet was rather distracting.

"I am going to need you to be quiet now, Lillian."

Her best friend, Lillian Michaels, did not say any more, but she also did not stop pacing.

Mary huffed out a breath. "Someone is practicing here in case you haven't noticed."

The shuffling stopped and Mary refocused her

aim. She drew out her bowstring as far as she could. Then…

"I think your feet are too far apart."

"Oh…" Mary stopped the epithet that had almost escaped her lips. She'd released at the same instant Lillian had spoken, missing the bullseye by quite a wide margin. Her eyes narrowed as she swiveled to face her friend. "I hope you're happy about that."

Lillian feigned a look of innocence. "I didn't think my words would distract you this much."

"That is the second time I've missed the bullseye because of you." Mary pointed the end of her bow at Lillian instead of her finger.

A smirk split across her friend's face. Oh, yes. It had definitely been deliberate.

"Are you positive that you should be blaming that on me?" Lillian asked. "Perhaps an honest assessment of your skill would be more appropriate."

"Why, you impertinent—"

"Mary." The voice of Mrs. Martha Goodings, the manager of the Boston Athletics Club for Women, interrupted their laughter. "May I have a word?"

There appeared to be an urgency about the manager, and the ordinarily cheerful lady had worry lines pronouncing themselves at the corners of her eyes and mouth. Her eyes were moist, too.

Replacing her bow on a nearby rack, Mary allowed Martha to pull her to the side of the room, but not before she caught sight of Lillian out of the corner of her eye, craning her curious neck.

"We appear to have a serious situation," Martha began. "Gertrude Fox is dead."

Mary's hand went up to cover her mouth. "I beg your pardon?"

Gertrude Fox was a wealthy and immensely popular lady. She was also one of the founders of the women's athletics club.

"It's terrible! Gertrude's body was discovered in the locker room some minutes ago by Lady Adele Belmont. I think she must have had a heart attack."

"A heart attack?" Since becoming apprenticed to her brother-in-law Henry in his private detective business, Mary's specialty was in investigating and solving crimes. She didn't understand why Martha would pull her to the side just to tell her about a natural death, as tragic as the news was. "Why do you need a word with me?"

Martha's eyes darted to the side, obviously to check if anyone was within earshot before she answered. "*I* believe she had a heart attack. The woman was nearing seventy, but my suspicion is merely that, suspicion. Lady Belmont believes something else."

Mary nodded. "All right. I'll have a look at her. Let's go."

Her heart pounded as she followed Martha out of the archery practice area. A dead body! She didn't want to show any hesitation, but had to admit to feeling rather nervous at the thought of what she was about to see.

They made their way to the locker room where Gertrude had been found. The building was already buzzing with activity that had less to do with women training, and more to do with what had happened. Mary was uncertain what to expect, but she kept her mind focused as they entered the locker room.

Lady Adele Belmont, one of the patronesses of the club, was weeping over the body, which was covered with a white cloth. Mary sucked in her breath as she approached, questions running through her mind. What if the cause of death had not been natural? Would she be able to tell, with her limited experience in detecting?

Lady Belmont stepped aside, wiping her eyes, and Mary crouched down beside Gertrude.

"May I?" she asked, reaching for the cloth.

"Of course, Mary," Martha replied, turning away a little.

Very carefully, she lifted the covering to reveal the woman's pale face. This was no longer the Gertrude she had known and appreciated. This was merely a physical shell that had housed her indomitable spirit. Something clenched in Mary's chest and she squeezed her eyes shut for a moment. When she opened them again, her gaze went straight to the small blood pool beneath the body's head.

"This blood…" She gestured with a query.

"I think it must be from the impact of her fall," Martha supplied, her face becoming even more pale. The sight disturbed her, naturally.

"I don't think so." Lady Belmont shook her head. She seemed calmer now, from several feet away. "I think there's more to this. If Gertrude did have a heart attack, as you say, I rather think she'd slump to the ground, and such impact might not be enough to make her bleed like that."

Lady Belmont had a point, and Mary was more inclined to believe her theory than Martha's.

"I'm going to check her body now," she informed the two women in the room with her.

"Please, go ahead," Martha said.

She lifted the head to look underneath. Blood and matted hair prevented her from assessing the wound properly, but it looked to Mary's eyes as if it had not resulted from a fall to the ground, but rather, from something small and, well...round. The edge was even, and there was nothing beneath her on the ground to indicate that she had gotten such a blow in the fall.

"I think maybe this was not the result of a heart attack," she announced. The confirmation horrified her, and yet, she couldn't help the tiny ripple of excitement that ran through her. Am I a bad person? she thought. Of course, it was devastating that Gertrude had suffered this way but, at the same time, they could very well be looking at a murder case here, and she might be the one to eventually solve it.

Mary had worked hard in the past three years since being apprenticed to Henry, even fighting for a coveted place at Boston University to learn valuable forensics science skills. The new science was only just opening up more widely, and an opportunity to utilize such knowledge had been a long time coming.

"Truly?" Martha gasped.

"Lock the door, Martha," Mary said. "The scene must not be disturbed. We may be looking at a crime here." She drew the cover further down, thinking out loud. "She is wearing a damp swimming costume. This could tell us a little about the time of death."

"How?" Martha asked, coming closer.

"Her locker is open." She pointed at the open locker with some of the contents having spilled out to litter the tiled floor. "She likely was about to change into her dry clothing when she was attacked." Mary felt the texture of the swimming fabric between her thumb and forefinger: cotton. "If she was attacked immediately after she came in from the swimming area, then I would surmise about an hour must have passed since her death. But we can't be certain until she's been checked by an examiner, of course."

"What happens now?" Lady Belmont asked, sniffling once again.

"I'll need to contact Detective DeHavillend. Do you have a telephone?"

"Yes, in my office," Martha said, striding across the room to the windows to pull down the curtains before shepherding the other women out of the room.

"Detective DeHavillend is your mentor, is he not?" Lady Belmont asked, following the women out and watching as Martha locked the door.

"Yes, he is. And he is a good mentor, too." Henry DeHavillend was also her brother-in-law, but she tried not to remind people of that too often.

Quite a number of the Boston Brahmins disagreed with her apprenticeship with the famous detective, but it appeared that Lady Belmont was a forward thinker. She would be, to sponsor an establishment such as the Boston Athletics Club for Women. "Oh, I am certain he is," she said. "It is wonderful to finally see women being offered some of the same opportunities as men to explore the world and carve their path."

When they reached Martha's office, Mary reached for the telephone handset and raised it to her ear. She dialed the number of the DeHavillend residence and waited for the operator to connect her, tapping her foot anxiously on the carpeted floor. At last, the butler answered.

"Bender, this is Mary Armstrong-Leeds. Is the Viscount in?"

"Yes, Your Highness," he replied in the slow manner that she always found aggravating, especially in times of urgency. "Please hold on while I fetch him."

"Please hurry, Bender. This is urgent."

"Of course, Your Highness."

While Henry DeHavillend was being located, Mary suggested to Martha that she return to guard the locker room door. The woman hurried away, and Mary thought back to the crime scene—she supposed she should call it a crime scene despite the uncertainty of the situation. There had been something odd by the window. What was it? The thought flittered away when Henry's deep voice greeted her.

"Mary. Are you all right? Bender said it was in relation to an urgent matter."

"Oh, hello Henry. Yes, I'm fine. Thing is, we have a case at the Boston Athletics Club for Women. It looks like it might be a murder case."

Mary heard Henry suck in a breath. "Who is it?"

"The suspect or the victim?" Her question was flippant, she knew, but she couldn't help it. Despite the gravity of the situation, levity was how she dealt with things when anxiety threatened to descend upon her.

"I don't have time for this, Mary. Who was murdered?"

"Gertrude Fox."

There was a long silence on the other end. "That is not good."

"No, it is not." They were both aware that the victim's popularity could complicate the investigation.

"I shall be right over," he said curtly. "Secure the scene if you can. And take care of yourself."

"Already done. And, of course I'll take care." She rolled her eyes at his protectiveness as the call ended. Lady Belmont turned a curious gaze her way.

"He is on his way," she confirmed to the club's manager and patroness. "In the meantime, I will return to examine the scene more closely." She picked up a pencil and a sheet of paper from the desk, then crossed the room to the door.

Lady Belmont's hand stopped her before she could open the door. Mary looked up sharply, perplexed at the interception.

"Do you think she was murdered, Mary?"

Only now, when Lady Belmont was standing very close to her, did she see how much effort the woman was putting into appearing collected. She knew the two women had been friends. This must be devastating for Lady Belmont.

Her voice was gentle when she answered. "I cannot say for sure before closely examining the scene, but I believe she was, Lady Belmont. She couldn't have sustained such a head injury from slumping to a perfectly flat floor."

"My thoughts exactly." The other woman nodded, swallowing. Eventually she said, "And please, call me Adele." Then she released her hold on Mary, allowing her to leave. Martha was in front of the locker room when they returned, and she accompanied Mary in.

"Maybe best if you stay out here," Mary said to Adele. The woman seemed happy to linger in the hall.

"That suits me. There's only so much I can take right now."

"I'm sorry."

"Promise me you'll see this case to a just conclusion."

"I promise, Adele."

Making her way to the window, and pushing the

curtain that Martha had drawn earlier to the side, she found a drop of blood on the sill. A very small, slightly smeared drop. She then checked the tiled floor for more blood. There was none. Perhaps the window had served as an escape route for the murderer. Mary scrawled the information on paper before checking the window for signs of forced entry. Sure enough, it was open a crack.

"How often is this window opened, Martha?"

"Every day, I believe. This is a locker room, after all, and ventilation is essential."

"Someone must have come in through here."

"Who could possibly have done this? And why?"

"Someone with positively nefarious intentions." Mary returned to the body and pulled down the covering. Only a coroner could tell what had really happened at the time of death, but still, she checked again, this time noting a bruise on Gertrude's wrist. Signs of a struggle?

By the time Henry arrived at the clubrooms a half-hour later, her sheet of paper was filled with notes.

"I should return to the club members. They are all gathered in the lounging area. I should see to sending everyone home." Martha excused herself and left.

"What do we have here?" Henry asked as soon as he entered the room, getting straight down to business.

Mary gave him a quick summary. "There's a

wound on the back of her..." Her words trailed off and her eyes widened at the sight of the young gentleman who walked in a minute or so behind Henry.

The young and very handsome gentleman, who completely ignored Mary's presence and strode directly to the body.

CHAPTER TWO

"*Y*ou were saying?" Henry raised inquisitive brows at her.

Tearing her eyes away from the handsome man, she blinked a few times, bringing her brother-in-law back into focus. Clearing her throat, she continued. "There's a wound on the back of her head. Looks like blunt trauma."

"What makes you certain it's blunt trauma?" The deep-voiced query came from the dark-haired, blue-eyed Adonis, who crouched beside Henry, looking down at the body.

"Excuse me?"

He turned his gaze toward her at last, looking from the top of her messy hair down to her shod toes. A sardonic smile curved his lips. "You seem certain. Did you check the body?"

Mary clenched her teeth and jutted out her chin. "Would I have reached that conclusion if I had not?

The wound is quite symmetrical in shape, and there is nothing on the floor or near the body that could have caused such a blow."

He lifted a wide shoulder in a shrug before returning his attention to the body. "Her wrist is bruised," he said. "She must have struggled with her attacker." He pointed with a long slender finger. "And here, she's been hit on her brow, too."

Mary squinted, noticing a faint bruise on the brow. How had she missed that? Annoyance began to stir in her chest, and she wasn't sure if it was directed at the young man in front of her, or herself.

Henry's eyes narrowed as he studied the bruise. He rose to his feet. "Let's begin studying the scene."

"Here." Mary pulled out the sheet she'd filled with notes from her dress pocket. "I made notes."

"You took notes?" Adonis shot her a look that was part incredulous and part condescending.

"Yes." Her hands settled on her hips, a challenging stance. "Do you have a problem with that?"

"No," he said, shaking his head. "It's just something amateurs do."

"*What*? Just who do you think you are?"

Henry chose that moment to speak up. "Mary, this is Detective Bennet Brown."

Ah, so this was the promising new apprentice protégé that Henry had recently taken under his wing. Her competition.

To the other man, he said, "My sister-in-law, Her Royal Highness, Princess Mary Armstrong-Leeds."

"Why do you have to introduce me as your *sister-in-law* first?" she challenged Henry, who only smirked. She looked at Henry's other apprentice. "Detective Brown, it's nice to finally meet you."

That was a lie. The man was in dire want of good manners, and right now he was trying to take over her case.

"A pleasure, Your Highness." He stood up and swept into an elegant bow.

Warmth crept up her cheeks from her neck and her lashes swept down for an infinitesimally short moment before her commanding personality took over. "I would prefer it if you address me as Mary. Your Highness is far too..." *Stuffy*, she wanted to say, but the man had already turned his attention away again.

She stuffed her notes back into her pocket, feeling quite disgruntled. "As I was saying," she said, "I have already made a study of the scene. The attacker appears to have gained entry through the window, and—"

"With all due respect, Your Highness," Detective Brown interrupted, "I don't think you should be involved in solving this case. You knew the victim. We don't even know if it's a murder case yet, and you are already talking about an attacker."

"Murder is quite apparent, according to my observations."

He held up a hand in a dismissive gesture. "*Your* observations. And you are…what…an apprentice?"

"Well, so are you!"

"Yes, but I have many years more experience than you."

Mary's eyes narrowed and she smiled at him without humor. "I'll have you know, Detective, that I have a science degree with a focus in forensics."

"Impressive, no doubt." He returned her smile. "But there is a limit to how much your esteemed degree can help you when you are wanting of experience."

"And you appear to be oozing that experience, Detective?"

He tugged down his vest. He was dressed in simple daywear: a gray morning coat with matching vest and trousers. "Certainly. I joined your brother-in-law's detective agency from the police. I have been working with them for a long time."

"Hmm." Mary tilted her head. "But there is a limit to how much your esteemed *experience* can help you when you are wanting of education, Detective."

Surprisingly, a grin split across his handsome face. "*Touché!*"

Her heart beat a little faster at the sight. To hide her reaction, she batted her lashes at him, forming her lips into a small sultry pout, hoping the employment of her feminine charms would fluster him.

He appeared to be immune.

"I still think your judgment cannot be trusted,

because you knew the victim in this instance," he said. "Detective DeHavillend might have another assignment for you, and leave this one to me."

"You obviously give yourself far too much credit." She rolled her eyes and laughed. "If your experience is so vast and credible, then why have I not heard of you before you started working with Henry?"

"Perhaps you've been too busy having a good time with your high-society friends?"

"Oh, so you're one of those." Her gaze swept over him, silently appreciating his chiseled features and broad shoulders, even as she felt her annoyance rise.

"One of what?" He folded his arms across his chest, the motion pulling his coat tight about his torso.

"The Brahmin Challengers."

The Brahmin Challengers was a title given by the press to members of the upper-middle class who challenged high society members, claiming their wealth and titles were unearned; and that they did not value or respect honest hard work.

He shrugged, showing neither affront at her words, nor interest in pursuing the topic. Most people who challenged the lifestyle of the elite would argue with her when she called them out. This man, Bennet Brown, was hard to decipher.

"I've been around for a while," he said at last. "It's not my fault you don't know every police officer in Boston."

"I—"

"*Enough!*" Henry cleared his throat. "That is enough, the both of you."

She straightened, her gaze meeting the detective's, silently telling him they were far from through with the conversation. His grin conveyed his acceptance of her challenge.

"There is enough here for me to declare this a murder case. Brown, you will contact the police captain and arrange for an autopsy at the coroner's office."

"Of course, sir." Without looking back at Mary, he exited the room.

"Why did you do that?" Her voice sounded sharp in her own ears and she winced. There was nothing she disliked more than sounding desperate.

"What did I do what?" Henry's wry smile belied his look of innocence. He knew what he'd just done.

"You handed my case over to him."

"It is not your case, and I did not hand it over to him. *I* am handling this case, and Detective Brown will be assisting me."

"And me?" She folded her hands across her chest and jutted her chin forward.

His hand came down on her shoulder. "You, my dear, will go home."

Mary unceremoniously removed his hand from her shoulder. "Do what at home, precisely?"

"Your mother might need you for something."

"Henry, I can't believe you are treating me this way. I insist you let me take the lead here. You know I have finished my exams and I am diligently working toward a career in criminalistics. You know I can do this."

A sigh was pulled from him. "Brown is right, Mary. You don't have enough experience to take this one on. Of course, I know you are highly capable. But murder? No."

Fury stirred in her chest, rising up to her throat and almost choking her. "Whose fault is it that I don't have experience?"

"Mary—"

"Who relegates my investigations to missing animals and the occasional theft, Henry?"

"You were studying, and needed to focus on your studies. Your brother would have killed me if you failed your exams because you were out following a lead. Remember how much effort it took to convince Penforth to allow you to study what you wanted."

Her face fell at that memory. Penforth had only agreed to allow her to study the sciences if she could prove she could hold her own and perform well.

"That is true," she acknowledged. "But I am qualified now, and ready to take on more. What was the point of studying, if I can't apply my new skills? Please, Henry. You need to let me take the lead." A timely thought pushed itself to the fore of her mind. "Besides, you don't have the time to lead on this, with Libby and your new baby."

Her sister had recently given birth to a beautiful

baby girl, and everyone was smitten, especially the baby's father, Henry.

He sighed again, and shook his head. "You're impossible, Mary. Sometimes I have trouble deciding which one of you is more stubborn, you or your sister."

A smirk settled comfortably on her face. "There's no winning against either of us, even more so when we're united."

A cautioning finger immediately came up. "Don't even think about it. You are not going to use Libby to convince me to let you solve this case. It's not going to work."

"It's worked before."

"*Before*, not now."

Mary groaned. "You're being unfair, Henry."

"Go home. The body will be moved once the police arrive."

Deciding to do what he'd advised—for now, and definitely without giving up her intent to investigate this case—Mary crossed the room to the exit.

"I'll see you at home," he called after her. She half-turned when he added, "Unless you decide to move back in with your mother, or with Pen and Anna."

I am not going to dignify that with a response, she told herself, reaching for the doorknob.

She was always moving between Henry and Libby's townhouse, and her brother Penforth's new home that he had set up with his lively wife, Anna.

Her mother, Christiana, normally lived with Pen and Anna, though at present she was also staying with Libby, due to the new baby. They all seemed to enjoy Mary's company, wherever she lived, but it was starting to feel a little tiring, bouncing around based purely on whim. One day, it would be nice to have a place she could call her own, and if she could make a go of detecting, perhaps that day may come sooner rather than later. Of course, her brother was wealthy enough to buy her a place of her own, should she ask. But she didn't want to rely on a man. She wanted to be able to support herself. The rights of women had come far, but they still had a long way to go.

She sighed as she hailed a carriage. One day, she would convince them all that she was just as capable as the next person.

It seemed she just had to beat Bennet Brown to the finish line, to prove that.

CHAPTER THREE

*B*ennet's eyes scanned the locker room for Princess Mary when he returned with the police, but only Detective DeHavillend was present. Pity. She was annoying, that one, but he had found himself strangely exhilarated while conversing with her. He opened his mouth to ask where she'd gone, but DeHavillend spoke first.

"You will be handling this case from now on, Bennet, with me overseeing you. You're good at working in the field by yourself, are you not?"

"Of course." He frowned, wondering how Mary had taken that news. He stepped carefully around the body to cross to the window where DeHavillend stood. Behind him, a police team was preparing to move the body, marking the outline with chalk.

"Good. I am working less recently, as you know."

"And Princess Mary?"

"Will not be involved."

"I don't think she'll be happy about that. She was quite vocal about wanting to be involved in this case."

A small smile softened DeHavillend's features. Bennet could tell he had a soft spot for the girl. "She will be fine."

Bennet thought DeHavillend was downplaying her reaction a little too much. To his mind, Mary would be very angry about being taken off a case she had already claimed as her own. But then, what did he know about her? He'd been in her company for less than half an hour.

Still, even in that short time, he'd discovered she was as decisive and strong-willed as she was beautiful. Those intriguing dark eyes had burned with challenge and passion when she spoke. He realized with a slight sense of shock, that he wanted to see her again.

"Brown?"

He snapped his attention back to the man in front of him. "Yes, sir?"

"I will take my leave now." Henry's eyes narrowed. "Be mindful of distractions."

Bennet did not miss the warning in his boss's words, and he suddenly wondered if Henry's reason for taking the princess off the case had more to do with keeping his two apprentices apart rather than her lack of actual experience.

A lick of guilt ran through him. As annoying as she was, Princess Mary did not deserve that.

Mary cycled home, her thoughts circling as fast as her legs. She kept trying to think of ways to convince Henry to allow her to work on the case. The door opened as soon as her feet touched the marble steps after parking her bicycle in the holder out the front of their townhouse. The butler must have been keeping an eye out for her. She bounded up the front stairs and Bender bowed as she entered. She inclined her head in a regal thank you.

The soft voices of her mother, sister, and sister-in-law fawning over her little niece, Amelia, greeted her from the foyer. Visitors, when she was not in the mood at all.

Then Treacle, her old brown cat, ran toward her, circling her legs and purring. No matter which house she was staying in at the time, Treacle always came with her, settling in well as long as Mary was there, too.

She reached down and stroked his fur. He purred more and closed his eyes but when she tried to pick him up, he resisted, turning with his tail up in the air and walking away as if all he'd wanted from her was to be stroked, and now that he'd gotten that, she no longer had use.

She smiled after him fondly, feeling a little better, and decided to join the others in the drawing room rather than sneaking off upstairs. It was impossible to conceal her bad mood, though.

"Good day, ladies," she said, going straight to her favorite chair and picking up a book from the side table, opening to the page she had marked with a velvet ribbon.

"Good day to you, too," said her sister-in-law, Lady Anna Trevallyn Armstrong-Leeds, smiling at her. "And what has you in such a mood?"

Mary shook her head and looked down at the open page without seeing it. "Nothing."

Anna raised a curious brow but a coo from Amelia drew her attention away. She took the baby from Libby and began to play with her.

"That is a very interesting book you have there, Mary," Libby observed in a wry tone. She was obviously trying to pry Mary out of her mood. Mary ignored her sister, until Libby added, "Who reads those kinds of books?"

She looked up then. "Someone striving to become a professional lady detective," she replied archly, slamming the book shut and turning it over in her hand. It was about the newest research into the study of fingerprints and bloodstain patterns. "Contrary to what you seem to believe, it's a very interesting book."

"Only to a detective," her mother, Christiana, teased.

Amelia gurgled, and Mary turned to look at the incredibly adorable child. She found herself smiling, despite her determination to wallow in her mood.

"Here." Anna stood and came over to her seat, placing the two-month-old baby into Mary's arms.

"You look like you could use a bit more joy right now. Joy only this little angel can give."

Mary settled Amelia in her arms and began to rock her, beaming down at her niece as she did so, and momentarily forgetting her troubles.

"Mama!" One of Anna's rambunctious toddlers ran squealing into the room. Rose clutched at her mother's skirts as her twin brother ran after her, drooling. The poor girl disliked it when her brother drooled. "Jewemy, thtop!" Her tiny hand came out from behind Anna to swat him. "I thaid, thtop!"

Libby pulled Jeremy toward her, laughing. "Stop scaring your sister, little man." She tickled him and he fell over giggling. This tableau, as beautiful as it was, made Mary aware of her mixed feelings about marriage and children. While she thought she might like this, one day, she was certain it was not what she wanted out of life at this point in time.

The governess who looked after Rose and Jeremy came rushing in then and marshaled the rowdy pair out, allowing the women to have some peace once again. Mary handed Amelia over to Christiana, and sat back down in her chair.

"Gertrude Fox is dead," she announced suddenly.

The room went quiet at the news, each woman's eyes widening with shock.

"When?" Christiana asked.

"What happened?" This came from Libby.

"Today, in the athletics club locker room. Murdered, I think."

Their collective gasps filled the room and Mary released a long breath, feeling terribly sad for the loss of Gertrude, and hoping she had found some peace, at least.

"What do you mean, murdered?" Christiana asked. One hand still cradled the baby, and the other was fluttering at her throat. She was quite well-acquainted with Gertrude, given they supported many of the same charities.

"When her body was found, Martha Goodings called me in to check the scene. She thought it might have been her heart, but Lady Belmont was there too, and she said she suspected foul play. Henry is on the case now."

"This is horrible," her mother whispered, still clutching at her neck.

"It is," Mary agreed. She gave a faint shudder at the memory of Gertrude's vacant features.

"Are you going to help with the case?" Anna asked.

Mary's lips thinned. "Henry won't let me." She cleared her throat, trying not to sound fierce, and failing miserably. She shrugged. "I am quite furious with him right now, to be honest."

"When are you not furious with him regarding a case?" Libby quipped, attempting to lighten the gloomy air in the room.

"Well, never, but that's not the point. He used my studies as an excuse to keep me off *real* cases. Now that I've completed my studies, he is still refusing to allow me to take on anything meaningful."

"Perhaps he thinks the work is dangerous?" Libby said.

She rolled her eyes. "You were accused of murder four years ago and you single-handedly solved the mystery and cleared your name, Libby."

"No, I cleared my name with Henry's help."

"Doesn't matter. My point is, *that* was dangerous and he still let you do it. I don't think danger is the full reason why he is preventing me."

"What do you think is his reason, then?"

"I'm uncertain. His excuse is my lack of experience."

Anna released a huff. "And whose fault is it that you lack experience? Oh, I'm annoyed on your behalf!"

"Thank you, Anna! I told him that and he still remained vehement. Ordered me to come home and help Mama with something." She gave her mother a sidelong glance. "No offense, Mama."

"Oh, none taken. You are far too much for me to handle, anyway."

"And do you know what is worse?" She was venting now. "He brought that new apprentice detective and put *him* on the case instead. He's been working with Henry for just six months...or even less, I think."

"Bennet Brown is your competition?" Libby stood

and walked to the bellpull near the fireplace to summon a servant.

"Yes." She felt no shame in expressing what some might perceive as pettiness. Not in this company. "He sounds like an upstart, claiming to be in possession of ample experience which he said trumps my education."

"Oh, dear," Anna murmured.

"He makes me mad just thinking about him. Oh, I hope you're ringing for refreshments, Libby." Food was always a nice panacea, and she could use some victuals at this time.

Libby pulled the bell. "Of course, I am. And... Bennet Brown is not as obscure as you think."

"Really?" Mary's eyebrow rose in query as she stared at her sister.

"Yes. I believe Henry said something about him having been a sergeant with the Boston Police for some time. An awarded one, at that."

Mary was not the least bit impressed by that bit of news. "He disregarded my education and took over as if he's already been given leave to lead the case. I didn't like it. It felt as if I was being dismissed because I am a woman."

"Have you tried talking to Henry?" Christiana had rocked Amelia to sleep, so she spoke quietly.

"I have. He won't listen."

Bender appeared in the doorway, his face the perfect example of placidity. Mary wished she could be as unconcerned about the world as he seemed to be. Libby ordered refreshments for them, and in gratitude, Mary's stomach rumbled slightly.

"I suspect you've been demanding. Henry is resistant to demands," Libby said.

Mary huffed out a breath, her frustration growing. "What would you suggest I do?"

"Use your charm instead. Every man has a natural sympathy for a woman no matter who she is."

Now Mary's other brow rose to join the other. "*Every* man?"

"You know what I mean. Every man with a heart."

"Not the monsters," she murmured to herself. Like the monster that had killed Gertrude Fox. But that could have been done by a woman. If the genders were to be truly considered equal, then everything—both good and bad—must apply.

"Appeal to that part of him."

"Is that how you do it?"

Her sister smirked. "He is my husband. I know how to persuade him if I need to."

Mary groaned. "Then help me convince him."

Libby shook her dark head. "You're on your own, my dear. Use. Your. Charm."

"That is horrible advice, Libby. Why must you encourage your sister to be involved in crime-solving?" Christiana had been listening to them without commenting until now.

She understood crime-solving was her youngest

daughter's passion, but she was yet to completely accept it.

"Mama, I'm only trying to help," Libby argued.

Her mother stared at Libby, and then turned to Mary. "I agree with Henry. You should not be involved in this case."

Mary sank deeper into her chair, her hands coming up to massage her temples. If her own family would not support her...

"I have an idea." Anna perked up, her blue eyes brightening. "Why not use what you've learned at the university to convince Henry to let you work on the case. If you present logical reasons, surely he won't deny you?"

Mary worried at her bottom lip as she considered Anna's suggestion. "I like the sound of using logic rather than charm, to be honest." She frowned, annoyed that she had not thought of this herself. But that annoyance quickly disappeared, as logical arguments ran through her mind. She shot to her feet, re-energized. "That might just work! Thank you, Anna."

Moving to the small writing desk in the corner of the drawing room, she sat on a chair and withdrew the pencil and her scrunched-up paper of notes. She straightened out the paper and turned it over, using it to write down why she was the perfect choice to take the lead on this case. Logical argument. She could be supervised by Henry...and supported by Detective Brown.

Her lips curved into a hopeful smile at the thought of the arrogant man being her support. They could all work together on this one, and she would show Henry once and for all that she was capable of becoming a full detective at last.

CHAPTER FOUR

That evening, Mary spent more time than usual dressing for dinner. She had two choices before her.

Wear her best dinner dress and style her hair flamboyantly. Or go for a severe look with less glamor. Her lady's maid, Minnie, held up two dresses: a stoic blue satin one, and a green silk one.

"Which would you like, Miss?" she asked. Mary could not convince her maid to call her by her first name, so they had settled on Miss as a compromise.

Mary took the blue satin dress and held it against her body in front of the mirror. "If I wear this, I will be taken very seriously. I will look intelligent and professional. Convincing Henry to let me work on the case should be easy."

"Or he will think you are there to interrogate him," Minnie said, giggling.

"Oh, imagine that!" She turned around with the

dress, shaking her head. "This reminds me of what I wore to my exams. You're right. It's *too* serious."

"Try this one." Minnie handed her the green silk.

"Hmm."

"You'll look ravishing in this one. If you were going to a social event, you'd surely draw a lot of attention. A proposal or two, even."

Minnie's words were met with a roll of Mary's eyes. "If anyone proposed now, I'd run away."

Mary's debut into society almost three years prior had been considered a success. Taken over by the social whirlwind, she had blossomed and come into her own. She had received more proposals than she could count and to her family's astonishment, had turned every one of them down. They'd not felt right at the time.

What *was* right, though? Would it ever arrive, and if it did, would she recognize it?

Mary was not sure. Her priority now was to feed her independent spirit, pursue her dreams, and become a detective.

"My dear Minnie," she declared, looking at her reflection. "I daresay the green wins. This brings out both my charm and intelligence."

"I know just what to do with your hair, Miss."

"Not too fancy, please."

"No, Miss."

Minnie helped her dress, then she sat down in front of the vanity table to watch as her voluminous dark hair was swept up and twisted into a coil atop her head. She didn't need curlers, for her hair possessed a natural wave that was very flattering.

Mary knew she was lucky in that regard, and appreciated her natural beauty.

"A bit of rouge?" Minnie tried to dab the rose color onto her cheeks but Mary ducked away.

"Now, that's a step too far."

"Then you are all ready, Miss."

Smiling broadly, she stood, feeling supremely confident, and took hold of the train of her dress. "Wish me luck, Minnie. Tonight may well determine my future."

"Good luck, Miss."

When she arrived in the drawing room, she found Libby and Christiana already on the sofa, and Henry standing by the fireplace, a glass of whiskey in hand.

"There you are! We were just talking about you," Libby sang, mischief in her eyes.

"Hmm. I hope you were saying good things?"

"Only the best, trust me." Libby gave her a small wink.

"She is trying to convince her husband to let you work on the case," Christiana said. "While *I* am trying to convince him otherwise."

Mary looked at Henry, actually feeling a little sorry for the man. "They're essentially pulling you from both sides. How do you feel about that?"

A satisfied smile crossed his face. "I have already made my decision, and nothing my wife or mother-in-law say will sway that."

Libby pouted and Christiana frowned. Mary simply stepped in to the suddenly quiet breach. "How about you give *me* a chance to state my case? I am not sure of your decision, but surely, as your apprentice, I deserve to be heard before you announce it?"

He raised a brow, waiting for her to go on.

"I have thought of many reasons why I am the right person for this job."

"Very well. Let's discuss it after dinner."

Mary almost shot up her arm into the air in triumph but she held back. She didn't want to be preemptive. He'd only given her a chance to present her case. There was still a battle to fight.

Bender appeared in the doorway to announce that dinner was served. They all filed out toward the dining room.

AFTER DINNER, HENRY EXCUSED HIMSELF TO complete some business paperwork. When he returned, he invited Mary into the library. Her heart thudded loudly in her chest. This moment was so important to her, but she wasn't sure if anyone else understood just how important.

Instead of sitting down, she stood in front of the marble fireplace while Henry sat in a chair. His fingers were steepled together.

"My first point is in relation to my experience, or lack thereof," she began. "Now, I know you are reluctant to entrust this case to me because of my lack of experience, but everyone has to start somewhere. Even you, Henry, and Detective Brown, once had no experience with large investigations. But I am smart, and a quick learner, and I have method and process under my belt already by working on smaller cases for the past three years."

He gave her a small nod, acknowledging her words. The gesture encouraged her to continue.

"Now it is time for me to scale things up. I sought education in criminalistics for a reason." She moved from the fireplace and paced back and forth across the room before ending up standing behind the chair opposite him. She gripped its back to steady herself. "I worked hard at my university studies so that I may employ my education in solving cases. I love this job, Henry. I want to be successful at it. If I can apply what I've learned, including some of these new areas of research, we can make breakthroughs we never would have thought possible a couple of years ago. Think about it. The world is moving very fast and I intend to keep up with it. I can be an asset to your team, not a liability."

Henry leaned back in his chair and studied her. "You've given this a great deal of thought, haven't you?"

"Of course, I have. This is my career, after all."

"Please, continue." He placed the ankle of one leg over the knee of the other.

She took a deep breath. "Detective Brown does

have more experience than me. Of course, he does. But that doesn't make him better than me at the job. It makes us different. I believe we *both* have skills to offer you, Henry, and perhaps we should both be involved. You—and Detective Brown, if it comes to that—can keep an eye on me to make sure I'm doing a good job and advise me accordingly. Your team will end up stronger because of it."

"I'll admit, you offer quite a robust argument."

Something lit up inside her when he said that and she stood a little straighter, holding her breath in her lungs. Until the next words out of his mouth made her huff it all out in a rush.

"I'd already decided to allow Detective Brown take the lead because of his experience."

Disappointment rushed through her. Her lack of experience might just be the undoing factor in her career. All she needed was one chance to prove herself. Just one chance! She closed her eyes and waited for him to finish crushing her dreams.

"He was a police sergeant for two years and has successfully solved some excellent cases."

"And he won awards, I know. How can I compete with that?" Mary mumbled to herself.

"But you were right to remind me of your education as a point of difference to Bennet. You do have formal training, and he has the experience. I think the two of you could do well working together. So, Mary, you have managed to change my mind. You will work together on the case of Gertrude Fox's murder."

She had to restrain herself from jumping up and down and shrieking with excitement. "You mean that? Really?" Hope, once again, bloomed within her.

He smiled warmly at her. Clearly, she had not hidden her reaction completely. "Yes, I mean it. But you are not taking the lead. You may work in partnership with Detective Brown."

"That is fine by me, Henry, for half a loaf is better than no bread at all. Oh, thank you!" She flounced around the chair and took a seat, scarcely able to sit still.

"You can use this opportunity to learn from each other, under my overall supervision."

"That sounds wonderful. I'll be at the Investigation Services Office first thing tomorrow morning."

"Just ensure you get a good night's sleep," Henry said with a chuckle. "I need my royal detective sharp and focused."

He was right. Though how she would be able to sleep tonight, was beyond Mary right now. Her mind was whirling with all manner of thoughts as she left Henry and ran back to the drawing room to let the others know that, come morning, she would be commencing investigation on her first major case.

CHAPTER FIVE

November 21, 1895

*M*ary assessed her appearance in the mirror one last time before setting out. Her high-necked shirtwaist, tucked into a midnight blue skirt and matching boots, lent her a professional air. Her nipped waist and dark voluminous hair under a hat turned up on one side spoke of her style, and her matching jacket her sophistication.

"Just like a Gibson Girl." Minnie sighed her approval.

"Quite so," Mary agreed, pleased at the comparison. "Though, with a New Woman's brain. Hopefully, at least."

She nodded at her reflection, then picked up her bag and went downstairs. Her bicycle was waiting at the front for her.

Her ride to the DeHavillend Investigation Services

Office—established over three years ago—did not take long. She took a moment to appreciate the building's red-brick facade when she arrived. It was not hers, of course, but she was still proud of it, knowing the work Henry had put into establishing the business after solving the Baroness Case, as people called it.

Henry and Detective Brown were waiting for her in Henry's office when she entered, and the sight of the young detective did not help to settle the flutter in her stomach.

"Good morning, gentlemen," she greeted, a broad smile gracing her features.

"Good morning, Your Highness." Detective Brown tipped his hat and bowed slightly. Her smile froze. She wasn't sure if his greeting was a form of respect or mockery.

"I told you that you needn't call me that." She inclined her head. "If we'll be working together, then I insist you call me Mary."

"Let's get to work," Henry cut in, giving Detective Brown a look she couldn't quite interpret.

"Here is what we know so far," Detective Brown began. "Gertrude Fox was definitely murdered. The examiner's official report will not be ready until later in the day or tomorrow, but my sources at the office have confirmed a blow to the head that was not accidental. The attacker possibly gained entry through the window, and likely left that way also. We do not yet have a suspect, but I have made a list of people we will need to interview." His eyes met Mary's then. "You are on this list, Mary."

She understood it was standard to question those people who had come into contact with the murder victim, but she was slightly affronted to find that he had added her name to the list. She perceived a silent challenge in the action.

"Of course, I am," she drawled, schooling her features to appear unconcerned. "I am a member of the club, after all, and I knew Gertrude."

"I'm happy we understand each other." He frowned, looking slightly perplexed.

"Don't tell me you expected me to argue?"

"I did, as a matter of fact." A smile tugged at one corner of his mouth.

"The two of you are going to be working together on this case." Henry looked from Mary to Detective Brown. "Your cooperation could determine your success or failure. I hope you will both keep that in mind."

"You won't have any issues with me." She looked squarely at Detective Brown when she spoke.

He shifted under her gaze. "Nor me."

"Good. You will both cooperate with the police, and I expect daily updates. I also expect to see both of you tonight at dinner." Henry's silvery eyes took on a mysterious glint. "You will then have the opportunity to demonstrate how you are going to approach this case. It will be a test of your work compatibility."

"We will be there," Detective Brown answered for them both.

Henry nodded and stood. "I will leave you now to sort out how you are going to handle this moving forward."

"You're leaving us in your office?" Mary asked. Henry loved this space. He often called it his second home.

"I am not. This is called a dismissal. I suggest you set up in one of the spare offices across the hall. Don't let me down."

She looked around the nicely featured room and smiled. Someday, she would have an office like this one. "We won't," she promised.

Detective Brown picked up the case folder from Henry's desk and started riffling through it before heading for the door.

Mary turned to follow him, but then stopped. "What will you be doing while we work on this case?"

Henry gave her a look that said she was being impertinent. "I think you should concern yourself with the task you were given, more so than my activities."

"I'm only asking in case you need help with another case."

He laughed then. "Mary, finish what is on your plate first before you ask for more."

He was right. Grinning sheepishly, she joined Detective Brown at the door and they proceeded to one of the empty offices in the building.

"How often have you been here?" Detective Brown asked, holding the door open for her.

She brushed past him. "If you are asking to further determine my suitability for this task, I regret to inform you that you are wasting your time."

"Must you always question my motive?" He followed her to a table and set down the folder.

Mary allowed herself an insouciant shrug. "Admit it, Detective Brown, you have been questioning my motive just as much."

"That is because I cannot quite read you."

Despite herself, the corners of her mouth tugged upward. "Are you saying I'm a mystery?"

"In a not-so-obvious fashion." His eyes flashed with something that looked like interest.

"Then I suppose I should keep you guessing."

"I do love the challenge that comes with a mysterious woman, but I doubt keeping me guessing for a long time will help either of us. You heard what DeHavillend said. We need to establish compatibility."

Mary could not help but laugh. "Don't you think openly expressing your desire to know me is very like showing your hand?"

He looked at her thoughtfully for a moment, then pulled out a chair for her. "It's a hand I would not mind showing you."

Her cheeks warmed as she sat down. "In answer to your question, I have been here quite a few times. Sadly, not as much as I would've liked."

"Ah, yes, you were occupied with your studies." He lowered his tall frame onto the chair beside her.

Any warmth or fluttering that had resulted from his flirting manner moments ago vanished. He was back to being his condescending self, the Bennet Brown of whom she was not very fond.

"While you were out hoarding experience so you could flaunt it in the face of the less privileged."

"You? Less privileged?"

"With respect to crime investigation, yes."

Detective Brown scoffed. "You were, and still are, being mentored by Detective DeHavillend. You have something no one else does, yet, you deem yourself less privileged."

"You are contradicting yourself, Detective. You think me unsuitable because of my experience, yet you think of my training with DeHavillend as a good enough qualification. Make up your mind, sir."

His cheeks tinged with red, but the obvious embarrassment faded quickly. However, she was delighted with the point she'd just scored.

Verbal sparring with Detective Brown was rather like archery, in a way. *And I just scored a bullseye, without really taking aim.*

"Shall we get to work, Detective?"

"Certainly, Your Highness."

Mary dismissed his address as a feeble attempt to annoy her, and opened the folder. "I will question the ladies at the athletics club that are on your list."

"That role has already been taken. Choose something else."

"They know me. They might be more forthcoming."

"Don't tell me you are unaware of how sentiment can get in the way of investigating."

"You don't have to worry about sentiment, Detective. I know what I'm doing."

Detective Brown pulled the folder away from her. "I have something here that suits you." He pulled out a paper. "You can write a full report of what we have so far. Start cataloguing the evidence—"

"Relegating me to office work while you have all the fun out on the streets, hmm?"

"You have to start from a level you can handle." His eyes met hers, glinting.

"That might have worked if you were in charge," she reminded him archly, "but we are equals here." She began to pull the folder back toward her but he, too, pulled from his side. "This is childish," she said.

After a bit more tugging, he relented, allowing her to have the folder. "I agree."

"How about we share most of the tasks. If we do them together, we can both be across every part of the process. We can compare notes as we go, and perhaps our differing viewpoints will throw some light along the way."

"Very well. We'll do that," he acquiesced. A soft smile came to his face then, stealing her attention once more. "Actually, that is a very good idea, Mary."

When he smiled like that, and finally said her name in a natural way, she forgot what about him aggravated her. They appeared to have formed a truce. There was no telling how long it would last, but she liked it. However, there was a competition between them that she should not underestimate. They might work well together, but Mary knew they would still try to outdo each other. They both wanted to impress Henry, after all.

"We can spend the morning reviewing what evidence we have, then interview the athletics club members after lunch. What do you think, Detective?" she asked, drumming her fingers on the table, hoping he would agree.

"I think...you should call me Bennet. We are working together, after all."

"All right. Bennet." She felt surprisingly shy saying his name, but it was nice to finally have a more normal element to their conversation.

"And I think that plan of action sounds good."

She gave him a slow smile in answer, before they bent their heads over the file on the desk and began to spread out the papers.

CHAPTER SIX

"Where should we have lunch?" Mary asked several hours later after glancing at the clock on the wall. It was well past noon.

"There's a small café about a block away from here. It's a nice establishment, especially if you have a sweet tooth."

"And do you think I have a sweet tooth?"

His eyes swept over her, leaving fiery trails in their wake. "There's only one way for me to find out."

They put the evidence, which they'd not been able to gain much from, away in a locked cupboard before gathering their coats and walking out of the building. The street bustled with life, infusing her with determination. Every person who walked past them had a story, a secret. One or more of them might know who murdered poor Gertrude...

Detective Brown took hold of her elbow, gently

pulling her toward him. She allowed the touch, enjoying it far too much. "It's this way," he said.

The walk took only a few minutes, and she found the café charming with outdoor seating available. "Would you prefer to eat in or out of doors?"

"Oh, out please. I love the fresh air."

Detective Brown's brows shot up in obvious surprise, before he led her to a table at one side of the outdoor area.

"I also like to observe people. Even when I'm eating, and that is far better done out here than tucked up inside," she added.

"What do you gain from that?" He pulled out a chair for her.

She gave him an incredulous look. "I'm a detective." He did not react to that, so she elaborated. "Knowledge. Body language often speaks far more loudly than words. Anyone can say anything, but the body sometimes has a mind of its own and provides a different message altogether. It is fascinating."

"Was that something you learned at university?" For the first time, Bennet's expression when referring to her education was that of genuine curiosity and not tinged with mockery.

"No, I began studying psychology before I attended university. Just by myself, from books. My brother's library is well stocked."

"I have a bit of a background in psychology as well." He called for someone to take their order. "Like you, I taught myself from books."

"It's interesting, the things we can learn on our own."

"Of course." He perused the menu and she did the same. After speaking a few words to the waiter, he turned to look at her, smiling a little. "So, tell me. Besides sitting in open spaces and observing people, what other peculiar pastimes do you have?"

"Peculiar?"

He shrugged. "You are not an ordinary woman."

"Is that a compliment I'm hearing?"

"More like an observation."

"Either way, thank you, Bennet."

He rested his hands on the table and leaned toward her. "I enjoy it when you say my name. You look slightly awkward, as if you're about to trip over the word."

Mary tilted her head to one side. "You enjoy my...awkwardness?"

"A little."

"Well." His steady regard made her cheeks hot. "At least you're honest."

He nodded, and asked her again. "So, what other peculiar pastimes do you have?"

"Clockmaking." If he was surprised by her response, he did not show it. "I collect rare broken pieces and put them back together. I have an entire collection."

"You are full of surprises." Another compliment? Bennet was generous when he allowed himself to be.

"I should like to see this collection of yours, if you'd let me. It sounds interesting."

"I can show you some of them tonight after dinner, if you like?"

"Only some?"

"Well, they are split into three." She felt another blush creep up her face. "Some are at my sister and Henry's home, some at my brother's, and some at my mother's apartment, though she is currently living with Libby and Henry and her own apartment is closed until next summer. I live in all three houses, you see, though I mainly bounce between Libby and Penforth's places."

"May I ask why?" he asked as their lunch was served.

"Whim, I suppose." She shrugged as she cut into her slice of pheasant pie. It was hard to explain why she didn't settle properly in one place or the other. Libby had found love and a happy life with Henry, and Pen was utterly smitten with Anna and their children. She sometimes felt like she was a little out of place in their happy family world. She wanted what they had, of course, but she wanted so much more out of life, too.

She placed a sizeable chunk of pie in her mouth. It was hard not to groan with pleasure at the explosion of flavor. When she glanced up at Bennet, his eyes were closed as he chewed. Apparently, he was enjoying the meal as much as she was. She smiled as she watched him.

He opened his eyes without warning and caught her smiling and staring. He dabbed at his mouth with a napkin, returning her smile in equal measure.

"Do you always do that when you eat?" she asked. "Close your eyes as if you're enjoying the best thing in the world?"

"I always have the best time when I'm eating," he said, taking another large bite and throwing a wink her way before closing his eyes again.

To her surprise—and delight—she enjoyed eating lunch with Bennet. He was intelligent, and excellent company when he was not telling her how his experience was superior to her education and social life.

"I've told you about my *peculiar* interests. Do you want to share any of yours?" she asked, finishing her meal and pushing her plate aside.

"It's only fair, I suppose, but I wouldn't call my hobbies peculiar. They're as ordinary as can be." He leaned back in his seat. "I love boxing. There was a time when I contemplated becoming a prizefighter but decided not to for the sake of my mother's sensibilities. She never liked it when I came home covered with bruises."

"I can imagine. Boxing is a great activity and I'm thinking of—"

"Boxing? You?" He laughed, interrupting her.

Mary tensed, her mouth forming a hard line. "Not boxing, but defense. I want to learn how to defend myself. It's important for women to learn, especially lady detectives."

"You don't need it, though. I don't see the point."

"Why not?"

Bennet waved his hand as if to swat away an insect. "The reality is, you are more likely to stay in the office."

And just like that, the nice interlude she had shared with him was gone. Pleasant Bennet, as she had dubbed him in her mind, had been replaced by the high-minded man she found barely tolerable.

"I thought we had an agreement about our roles. Surely, you do not think I will remain in the office while you have all the fun investigating. This case might take us to unsavory places, and I need to be prepared for anything."

He pursed his lips, and then gave her a curt nod. He didn't like it, but it seemed he had received her message.

"Shall we return to work?" she asked, deciding to put what had just happened behind her, though now she didn't feel at all like smiling at him.

"Yes." He stood, surprising her by offering his arm.

She took it gracefully and they walked up the street to hail a carriage that would take them to the Boston Athletics Club for Women.

Bennet understood that being DeHavillend's protégé meant that he'd have to meet and work with Mary. He just had not expected to be this affected by her presence. Something about her put him on edge, and yet he found himself inclined to get closer to her. Far closer than he wanted to admit.

"You said you wanted to interview me." She took the hand he offered and he helped her step down from the hired carriage.

"Yes, but your interrogation will have to wait until we have finished here with the others."

A sly smile curved her pretty lips. "You were very eager this morning."

"And you were not. I wonder what brought on this change."

"Perhaps I know something." Her dark eyes glimmered with challenge.

"Frankly, I doubt that. You know just about as much as I do."

"You sound very certain," she said archly, leading the way into the Boston Athletics Club for Women.

Bennet laughed and followed. "If you knew more than me, you would have played that card by now to gain a point against me."

An older woman was standing behind a desk in the front hall, gathering sheaves of papers. When she saw them, she smiled, but the effort was half-hearted. "Good afternoon, Mary. Mrs. Goodings is expecting you, since someone from Detective DeHavillend's office telephoned earlier."

"Good afternoon, Cecile." Mary approached the desk and turned to Bennet. "This is my partner, Detective Brown."

"Good day, Detective," Cecile greeted.

He nodded in return.

"The club is temporarily closed, of course, while the investigation is going on, but Mrs. Goodings is in her office. I've just been in sorting some paperwork, but I will be leaving soon, however."

"Can we ask you a few questions before you leave, Cecile?" Mary asked.

"Of course. Anything to help the law. Gertrude was good to all of us. A terrible business. Terrible." Her eyes clouded and the woman sniffed back a sob.

He could tell that the death of Gertrude Fox had affected the woman but she was trying to put on a brave front and get on with things in a normal way. A little bit like Mary, he realized with a sense of shock. His fellow detective was focusing hard on the investigation, perhaps in part to avoid the sadness of losing someone she liked.

Mary turned to him now, and his gaze softened at the determination he read on her features. "Over to you, Detective," she said.

"Right." He retrieved a small leather-bound book from his coat pocket and pulled out the tiny pencil from the spine. "How long had you known Gertrude Fox?"

"About four years," the woman answered. "Since I started working in this establishment."

"What can you tell us about your relationship with her? Did you like her?"

"Oh yes! She was lovely. Though we were only at the level of acquaintances, really. Mrs. Fox had a small circle of friends, but she was a very nice and cultured woman." Her eyes misted as she spoke. "She was kind and generous to all of us working here at the club. She believed in advancing the rights of women, and we were all grateful for her strength and support in that area."

Beside him, Mary released a shaky sigh. He glanced at her but her face betrayed nothing. He wanted to reach out and squeeze her arm to show his support, but he managed to restrain himself. That action would not go down well, he knew.

"In the days leading up to her death, did you notice anything unusual about her?"

Cecile shook her head. "Absolutely nothing. She was her usual cheerful self. She came here three times a week to swim. She loved swimming. I didn't notice anything unusual."

"Did you see her yesterday, before…"

Cecile nodded. "Yes, I was on the telephone when she arrived, so I waved her straight through. It was her usual arrival time, nothing out of the ordinary. She…she…"

The woman's bottom lip began to wobble dangerously, so Bennet cleared his throat and cut across her. "All right, thank you for your assistance, madam."

He took a moment to finish writing everything down and then gave her a small smile to express his condolences. "We will see Mrs. Goodings now."

He'd already interviewed the manager yesterday, but there were a few more questions he needed answering.

"Of course. Mary, do you need me..."

"No, I can take it from here, Cecile. Thank you."

The woman rushed away, scrubbing at her eyes as she went. Now it was Mary's turn to clear her throat. "This way," she said, and if her voice was a little wobbly, Bennet pretended not to notice.

Mary took his arm and steered him down a hallway to a door at the end.

She raised a slender hand and gave the door a soft knock.

"Come in," a voice called from inside.

She opened the door and walked in with him following.

"Oh, Mary!" Mrs. Goodings rose from her chair behind the desk. "It's so good to see you. Please tell me you really are working on the case."

"I am."

"Thank goodness." Mrs. Goodings' hand came up to flutter at her chest and her face brightened. "When Detective DeHavillend's office confirmed you might be working on the case, I was initially not happy. I don't like to think of anything bad happening to you as well. But now I am glad you are. I know how smart you are, and how determined. It gives me some peace of mind knowing you're here."

Reluctantly, Bennet admitted to himself that having Mary here with him was a good idea. The ladies appeared instantly more comfortable in her presence. Yesterday, his discussion with Mrs. Goodings had been stilted and awkward.

But he would not admit that to Mary, because then he'd never hear the end of her gloating.

"I am glad I'm here, too, Martha," Mary said. "You know Detective Brown, of course. He just has a few more questions for you, if that's all right?"

"Yes, of course." The woman nodded, and motioned toward the two chairs in front of her desk. "Please sit down."

After seating himself, Bennet began. "You said that you've known Gertrude for almost fifteen years. Can you think of anyone who might have had something against her?"

"That's the thing. Gertrude was so good to everyone. I can't think of a single person who would wish to harm her. And yet, someone did." Her pained eyes flicked in Mary's direction. "I still can't believe this has happened. The club is supposed to be a safe place for women to explore their athletic side."

Mary reached across the table to place her hand on top of the other woman's. Something in him softened at the sight of that gesture. DeHavillend had a reputation as one of the best detectives in America, but he was known more for the efficiency and indifference with which he carried out his interviews.

He had assumed Mary would be more like him, but she wasn't. She had a caring side, and clearly empathized with Mrs. Goodings, and previously, with Cecile.

Perhaps she showed empathy because of her acquaintance with the women they'd spoken with.

"Mrs. Goodings, you are the manager of this establishment so I expect you know all of your members. Is there anyone that you are not sure about? Anyone you can think of who might be inclined to do something like this? Anyone with a bad temper, or a jealous streak, or…"

He let his voice trail off, allowing her a moment to consider any and all possibilities.

She frowned at him. "Our members go through a thorough screening process before they're granted membership. I do not believe any one of them is capable of such an act."

"You must have a lot of faith in them."

"As a matter of fact, I do."

He nodded, reflecting on what she had said and feeling his frustration rise. So, they had no motive, no suspect and no lead. Solving this might take longer than expected.

"And the murderer used the window to escape, according to your observations," Mrs. Goodings said. "Every member who signed their arrival yesterday also signed their departure at the front desk. Everyone, except Adele—Lady Belmont."

Bennet straightened. "And why did Lady Belmont not sign her departure?"

"She was too distraught."

"She found the body, did she not?" His tone was a little more forceful than he intended and Mrs. Goodings raised her brows at him. Mary turned sharply to look at him.

"Lady Belmont is a patroness of the club," Mary said quietly. The cautious tone reminded him to be careful. He ignored her and focused on Mrs. Goodings.

"Yes, she did find poor Gertrude," the older woman said.

"Have they ever disagreed on anything? Especially regarding matters of the club?"

"Detective, you cannot think that she is anything but honest. She and Gertrude were good friends. They worked together to found this establishment."

"I understand, Mrs. Goodings. But I need to ask these things." In his notebook, he made an entry about interviewing Lady Belmont as soon as he could. Preferably without Mary around. "That's all my questions for now. Thank you." He stood, turning to Mary.

"I will catch up with you," she said. "I need a moment with Mrs. Goodings."

He raised a questioning brow.

"I will join you shortly," she said firmly, her dark eyes brokering no dissent.

"Fine." With a peremptory nod, he crossed the room to the door, wondering what it was that Mary wanted to talk to Mrs. Goodings about that she didn't want him to hear.

He knew she wouldn't do anything to jeopardize the case, like protect a guilty party; this investigation was too important to her. But he was curious, nevertheless.

When she joined him in the hall five minutes later, he asked, "What did you discuss?"

"Suspicious, are we?" Her eyes flared in that manner they did whenever he said anything she was not happy with.

"I trust you." And surprisingly, he realized he meant it. He *did* trust her. "I only wish to be kept apprised, if it is information that affects the case."

"It doesn't involve the case, I assure you. I only cleaned up after you. Your insinuation was not missed, and Lady Belmont is a very influential person in Boston society."

Bennet raked his hand through his hair. "Mary, I am a detective. I have to examine everything very closely, even those things that may not be palatable to you."

"Yes, of course. But there are more subtle ways of going about things."

"We're dealing with a murder. *Anyone* can be guilty here. Subtle doesn't cut it."

She stepped toward him, her expression softening. "I know, Bennet. I'm just suggesting you go at this in a gentler manner. These women have just lost a friend, and they are especially sensitive right now."

She had a point. He hadn't really thought of it like that. "All right, I will try. Though subtlety isn't really my specialty."

She smiled then. "You are not wrong there."

As they exited the club building onto the street, he offered her his arm. "It appears we're done here. Would you like to return to the office or go home?"

"Shall we not arrange to interview Lady Belmont?"

He cleared his throat. "Leave that with me."

She frowned up at him. "Right. Then I believe I will head home."

"Allow me to escort you."

She quickly shook her head. "I…err…I have to stop on my way to buy some lace. I don't suppose you fancy shopping for lace with me?"

That pulled a chuckle out of him. "I think not. By all means, spare me that torture."

"Good. I will see you tonight at dinner, then." She released his arm and hurried off down the street on her own.

CHAPTER SEVEN

*M*ary stood waiting for the streetcar to arrive, her boot tapping lightly on the cobbled ground. She had told Bennet the truth, about trying to smooth things over with Martha back in the office, though she suspected he had not done the same for her in relation to her suggestion to interview Lady Belmont.

It was frustrating, when he still obviously saw her as a fashion-obsessed girl rather than a fellow detective. If he did not ask her along to the interview with Lady Belmont, then she'd just have to go on her own.

Right now, though, she had another appointment, and it was definitely not to shop for lace. She couldn't imagine anything more boring, and in fact had more lace at home than she knew what to do with. Instead, she was going to find Drysdale's Gym and Boxing Hall. She had seen several of their flyers pasted on building walls, plus advertisements in the newspaper, advertising self-defense lessons for women.

Fishing in her skirt pocket, she pulled out the advertisement that she had cut out of a newspaper some days ago, a determined smile touching her features. She had been contemplating whether or not to go, but after Bennet's comments at lunch, had decided to locate the place and enroll.

Yes, the Investigation Services Office had a gym in the basement, but she had been challenged by Bennet. And Mary was not one to back out of a challenge.

The streetcar that would take her to the other side of the city arrived and she climbed in, holding a pole for support instead of sitting.

"Isn't it marvelous, Mary?"

Her head swiveled in the direction her name had come from to find a man and a woman talking animatedly.

"I cannot believe I've never been on one of these," the woman breathed, looking around the streetcar interior. "I've been so afraid. I mean, a horseless carriage that moves on tracks like a train, and is operated by electricity…" She shook her head as if she were supremely marveled by the conveyance. "This is amazing, Jack."

"The world is moving at an unprecedented speed, my dear."

Mary couldn't help joining in. "I felt the same the first time I rode in one of these," she said. "I was just as fascinated as you."

They looked at her, surprised. But then the expression on their faces turned pleasant.

"Were you filled with nerves before you got on?" the woman asked.

Mary chuckled. "I was. I didn't know what to expect. I thought it might take off while I was halfway in and I would end up sprawled in the street with my petticoats showing."

The man looked shocked at her words, but the women shared a grin. "Did you ever get used to it?" the woman asked her.

"Yes. It's become quite ordinary to me now."

"See?" the man said. "I told you there is nothing to be nervous about."

"I'm Mary Newfield, and this is my husband Jack Newfield."

She laughed. "What a coincidence. My name is Mary, too. Mary Armstrong-Leeds."

"Oh! Princess Mary?"

"Err...yes...that would be me." Her eyes narrowed. "How did you…"

"Oh, we read the society papers, and Princess Mary is mentioned there quite a lot. Especially your aspirations of becoming a lady detective."

Mary liked to think she was already a lady detective, or even better, a detective who happened to be a woman. But clearly, that wasn't the popular opinion. Yet.

"I had no idea I was mentioned that often." She knew she was in the papers more than her peers, but didn't think she'd be recognized immediately she mentioned her name.

"Oh, you are. And now I can tell my friends that I met Princess Mary."

"In a streetcar," her husband pointed out. "Talking about…ahem…undergarments, no less. I think they will hesitate in believing you."

Mary Newfield beamed. "That is why you're bearing witness, darling." They gazed tenderly at each other, and the conveyance slowed and then stopped at that moment. They stood. "We disembark here. It was so lovely meeting you, Your Highness. Good luck with the detecting."

"It was lovely to meet you, too, Mr. and Mrs. Newfield. Do have a nice day." Mary waved at them.

The Newfields appeared to be middle-class rather than from the upper echelons of Boston society, and yet still they knew of her. The thought set Mary's mind racing. Perhaps she really could use her social standing to influence people; bring change. If she could solve this case and gain the recognition she'd been working toward for years…show people that women could achieve whatever they set out to do just as well as men…

Hope swelled in her chest and her dream appeared just that little bit closer.

When the streetcar stopped, she hopped down, whistling. Her mother would clutch her chest in horror if she heard her daughter whistling.

After she'd walked several yards, she paused to

properly take in her surroundings. This was precisely the sort of place gently-bred ladies were discouraged from visiting. The streets were dark, not only because the sun had moved lower on the horizon, but because everywhere she looked was coated in dust and dirt. The further she walked, the more squalid everything appeared.

Perhaps this idea had been a little ambitious?

She tugged the lapels of her jacket closer and adjusted her gloves, trying to hide her nerves. Her shoulders straightened as she became more alert. How apt for a gym that taught women self-defense to be located where it might be needed.

A couple of blocks later, she arrived at a building that looked like a warehouse. The windows were situated too high for her to peek through beforehand.

"What in God's name are you doing, Mary?" she muttered to herself, summoning the courage to push open the rusted iron front door.

No sound could be heard from the outside, but once in, the sounds rushed over her all at once: grunts, heavy breathing, fists meeting with flesh. Then her eyes took in the scene: women of all shapes and sizes, in various states of undress. Goodness!

She spotted one or two women in proper gym costumes, but the others were only in their bloomers and corset covers. Her cheeks heated. Then a woman whose legs were flying through the air in swift kicks at a dummy caught her attention, and her embarrassment faded a little. She wanted to learn how to do that.

On the other side of the large space was an even more surprising sight. Men were fighting bare-chested, sweat spraying from their bodies and the sinewy cords of their muscles contracting and relaxing with every landed punch. Taking her eyes off them proved to be impossible. She was equal parts enthralled and repelled. She winced at a particularly hard punch by one man against another, his face contorting with the force as blood and saliva spilled from the other man's mouth.

She swallowed, hard.

"This place is not for the faint of heart," a woman called, approaching her. "Are you sure you're in the right place, Miss?"

Mary stood straighter and clasped her hands in front of her. "Of course, I'm in the right place."

The woman raised skeptical brows, looking Mary over. "I mean no offense, Miss. You look very fashionable, that's all."

"I will take that as a compliment. Are you Mrs. Drysdale?"

"Correct guess." The woman stood in front of her, tall and strong, and held out her hand. "Bridgette Drysdale." She turned her head and pointed with her chin at the man in the boxing ring who had thrown the vicious punch. "And that is my husband, Edgar. We run this establishment together."

"This is an interesting place you have. I saw your

advertisement in the paper a few days ago and want to enroll."

"I can't say I am not surprised. We don't often receive patronage like this. May I have your name please, Miss?"

"Mary...um...Mary Leeds." Revealing her true identity here might not be the smartest course of action.

"Welcome to Drysdale's Gym, Mary. What would you like to enroll for?"

"Self-defense," she answered, excitement building in her chest.

"My husband takes care of that course." She raised her hand and beckoned her husband over. "Edgar!"

The burly man ceased attacking his sparring partner and picked up a towel that he used to wipe the sweat from his face and neck before joining them.

"This is Mary Leeds," Mrs. Drysdale introduced. "She wishes to enroll in our self-defense lessons."

Mr. Drysdale held out a large hand and Mary shook it. "You've come to the right place. Not bragging but you won't find anything better in the whole of Boston."

"That's why I'm here, Mr. Drysdale. When can I begin, after taking care of the formalities, of course?"

"Whenever you wish. You can discuss the financial side with my wife."

Mrs. Drysdale took over from him. "You can try us out before you commit to anything. We offer the first session at no cost, and then after that, you can decide if we are a good fit for the course."

Mary had every intention of committing, but it wouldn't hurt to go through the trial first. "All right. Can I have the first session now?"

Mr. Drysdale nodded. "I will be over there by the punching bag when you are ready." He left them.

Mary looked around the room again. "Is this how you always train, barely dressed?"

"Yes, but it is not a requirement. Our clients are free to wear whatever they feel the most comfortable in. The ladies in their undergarments feel most unrestricted. But in some ways, it would be good to wear what you normally do, especially for the self-defense classes. It isn't like you'll have the chance to strip down first if someone does attack you on the street."

True, Mary thought. This was so very different from her athletics club where everyone wore a proper gym costume or their normal street clothes. Taking off her jacket and hat and setting them aside, Mary gave Mrs. Drysdale a nod and strode confidently to the waiting punching and the bare-chested Mr. Drysdale.

"Are you ready?" he asked.

"As ready as I'll ever be."

"Good. Let's begin." He stood between her and the punching bag and studied her stance. "Try standing with your feet wide apart, about the width of your shoulders." She did as he showed her.

"Remember, if they are too far apart or too close together, you'll lose your balance, and then you'd be knocked over more easily."

"That would be a shame, now, wouldn't it?"

Mr. Drysdale grinned. "I like your spirit."

"Thank you."

"Now, show me your fists." When she balled her hands, he nodded in approval. "Most beginners don't know how to make a proper fist. You've got your thumbs out instead of tucked in. That's good." He stepped away from her and faced the punching bag. With quick, agile movements, he gave the bag three fast successive punches. "Try that."

Mary released a slow breath, reining in her focus. Then she jabbed her fists at the stuffed leather bag, surprised at how hard it was.

"That's it!" he encouraged her. "A little bit more push through the upper arm, and you've got it. Jab fast, and hard. Also, keep breathing while you punch. You're a natural."

"Of course, I am!" Despite her bravado, she was inordinately pleased at the praise.

He showed her a new technique that involved kicking and she repeated it, her confidence growing with each successful hit.

Then a scream pierced the air, causing her head to turn in the direction of the sound. With her concentration robbed, the punching bag she'd just kicked returned to her, knocking her to the ground.

Mary landed on her rear end with an oof of breath escaping.

The rumble of Mr. Drysdale's laughter reached her and she looked up, massaging her smarting chin.

"Get cocky and *that* happens," he teased.

"I lost concentration because of the scream," she excused, her cheeks heating with embarrassment.

"Lesson one learned. You mustn't allow yourself to lose concentration in the first place. Or you'll find yourself with bruises all over."

"Hmm."

He offered her a hand to help her to her feet. "But you've done well for a novice. Good job."

"Oh, that chin is going to bruise," Mrs. Drysdale said, coming to join them. "Your posterior might be sore as well."

A small laugh rushed past Mary's lips. "I can feel that already."

"So?" Mrs. Drysdale's hands settled on her hips. "What do you think?"

"I'm definitely interested."

"Even with the chin?" she quipped.

Mary laughed. "Even with the chin. Sign me up, Mrs. Drysdale."

The woman beamed. "Follow me."

"Thank you for a good first impression," she called to Mr. Drysdale over her shoulder. He responded with a gesture of salute.

"How many lessons would you like to take?" Mrs.

Drysdale led her to a desk in a corner of the massive room.

"How many would you recommend?"

"I'd suggest six for a start. We'll see if you need more as we go."

"That sounds great." Mary paid for six lessons and a schedule was made for her; two lessons a week.

It was past sunset now and she didn't know the fastest route to the streetcar stop, so she asked Mrs. Drysdale about it.

"I can have my daughter show you the way. Give me a moment, please." Mary waited patiently as she exited and returned shortly thereafter with a young girl. "This is my daughter, Jenny."

"Good day." The girl smiled.

"Jenny will walk you to the tramcar stop."

"But she's so young to be out..."

"Oh, Jenny's had self-defense lessons practically since before she could walk. Plus, we're known in this area. No one would dare touch our girl."

"All right, then. Thank you, Mrs. Drysdale. Good night."

With every movement of her jaw, her chin ached, but she was thrilled. The feeling of strength and control her short match against the punching bag had granted her was like no other feeling she'd ever experienced.

She followed the younger girl down the street. "How old are you, Jenny?" she asked, curious.

"Fourteen."

"And did your parents train you?"

"Oh, yes. Me and my three brothers. Pa says he wants strong children that can take care of themselves in the world."

"That is very good. I'm here because I want to be strong."

Jenny's sharp green eyes assessed Mary. "You're not from this side of town. Why would you need to?"

"I'm a lady detective," she replied.

Jenny gasped and stopped short.

CHAPTER EIGHT

"Y ou're a lady detective?" Jenny asked, her face the picture of incredulity.

"Yes, I am," Mary said with a grin. They continued walking.

"That is impressive. What sort of cases do you work on?" Jenny shoved her hands into her jacket pockets.

"Theft, missing people and animals, murder—"

"Murder?" Jenny's eyes were as round as coins.

"A woman at the athletics club I attend was murdered, and I am one of the detectives on the case." She felt proud saying the words out loud. "Do you know Detective DeHavillend?"

Jenny guffawed. "Oh, who doesn't know Detective DeHavillend? His reputation is amazing."

"I work with him. He trained me, actually."

"Oh, this is inspiring!" The girl sighed. "Perhaps

we could work together. I like investigating, especially finding out information."

She had Mary's full attention now. "Go on."

"I can find information for you when you want." She smirked. "For a small token, of course."

"Of course. Clever girl. You have an eye for business, Jenny."

Jenny stood a bit taller, pleased. "Thank you, Miss Leeds."

"You're welcome. And yes, I would like to work with you."

Pulling her hand out of her pocket, Jenny held it out. They sealed their agreement with a handshake and a couple of coins.

It seemed Mary had achieved quite a bit today, including finding herself an information gatherer.

She gave Jenny her address when they reached the streetcar stop. "If I'm not home, you can leave a message with the butler. His name is Bender. I will tell him to expect you."

"See you, Miss Leeds." She waved as Mary hopped onto the streetcar, and skipped off down the street as Mary rolled away toward home.

BENDER LET HIS STOIC DEMEANOR SLIP WHEN HE SAW Mary. His mouth dropped open and his eyes went straight to her chin, so she knew it must have started to turn purple. She wiggled her brows at him. "Nothing to see here, Bender."

"Of course, Your Highness." He closed the door. "Would you like me to summon Minnie for you?"

"You are a treasure, Bender. Thank you."

Mary began to maneuver her sore body up the stairs. Her shoulders and thighs ached, her rear end was rather sore, and even her knuckles hurt. She was sure she'd feel even worse in the morning. "Bender?" She stopped on the second step and turned slightly.

"Yes, Your Highness?"

"A young girl, Jenny Drysdale, might be visiting, perhaps regularly. I work with her so she is always to be allowed in."

"Understood."

"And hand me that newspaper, please."

He picked up a copy of the day's paper from a table in the foyer and gave it to her. Mary thanked him with a wan smile before continuing upstairs.

Dinner time was approaching and she had to start getting ready. While she waited for Minnie to come up to her room, she walked into the dressing room and opened her closet, picking out two dresses at random. She tossed them onto the bed and flopped onto the mattress beside them with a weary sigh.

What a day she'd had.

"Good evening, Miss," came Minnie's voice as the door opened.

"Minnie, I need a bath. A very hot one." She

propped herself up on her elbows. "Massage oils for my shoulders, too."

"My, what have you gotten up to today to need massage oils?" Minnie moved to the window to draw the curtains shut. When she turned around, she gasped. "Oh, my Lord!"

Mary laughed, the movement causing her chin to ache more. "Don't look so shocked. This is not the first time you're seeing me with a bruise."

"Yes, but not as big as this one. And on your beautiful face! The thing is already purple."

"Don't I look pretty?"

Minnie shook her head, her mouth twisting in silent scolding. "We're going to have to cover that with creams and powders."

"Do what you must, Minnie." She flopped back onto the bed, confident in her maid's ability to conceal her bruise.

"I'll run the bath now." She disappeared into the dressing room leading to the bathroom.

Mary sat up with a grunt and reached for the newspaper. Gertrude's murder had made the headlines, as expected.

"How did you get hit on the chin anyway?" Minnie returned.

She held up a silencing finger until she finished reading.

"Can you believe what they're saying? Listen to this: *Gertrude Fox has been murdered in the most gruesome manner at the Boston's Athletics Club for Women. She was found nearly unrecognizable by the esteemed Lady Adele Belmont.*" She looked up at Minnie. "Nearly unrecognizable? That is a lie."

"You know how gossips are. They talk without facts. And those newspaper people…" Her maid screwed up her nose.

"Quite," Mary agreed, remembering how they had crucified her sister Libby, labelling her a murderer several years ago. The retraction had been a lot smaller and a lot further in than the front page.

"We should get you ready for your bath. The tub is filling fast."

Mary followed Minnie into the dressing room, still holding the paper.

"Hmm. They mention Henry's involvement in the case but not mine or Bennet's."

"The case is still new," Minnie said, undoing Mary's corset laces.

Mary continued reading in the tub, wondering how it could be that no one seemed to have any inkling of why Gertrude had been targeted. The entire front page and three columns of the second page revealed nothing, except further proof that Gertrude had been loved by all who knew her.

She was feeling more relaxed by the time she finished her bath. Minnie waited for her in the dressing room, and she'd already chosen one of the evening dresses that Mary had pulled out: a powder blue satin and lace dress with a tiny waist and a low but modest neckline that bared her shoulders.

"Excellent choice, Minnie."

She curtsied. "That is my job."

Minnie massaged Mary's stiff shoulders with some oil before helping her into the dress.

"I went to Drysdale's Gym this afternoon to take self-defense lessons," she explained to her maid. "It's how I got the bruise."

Minnie looked at her through the mirror, slowly shaking her head. "I suppose I'm going to be covering things like this until your lessons are over."

BENNET WAS SHOWN TO A BRIGHT AND SUPERBLY decorated drawing room when he arrived at the DeHavillend residence. He folded his large frame into a chair and waited for company. It did not take long to arrive.

"Evening, Brown," DeHavillend greeted, walking into the room with his wife, the Baroness Esk, on his arm. She smiled at him, looking a lot like Mary.

Bennet bowed courteously.

"I've never had the chance to introduce you both properly," DeHavillend said. "This is my wife, Her Royal Highness, Princess Elizabeth Armstrong-Leeds. Though she prefers to be known as Baroness Esk."

"Henry," the baroness chided. "You know I prefer Libby. Please, Detective, call me Libby. *I* would prefer it."

"Thank you, ma'am. I mean, Libby." Bennet bent

over her gloved hand and placed a light kiss on his hostess's knuckles.

"A pleasure, Detective Brown. I've heard quite a bit about you from my husband."

"Good things, I hope."

"All good, I assure you." DeHavillend led her to a sofa, and as she sat down, they exchanged a tender look.

Bennet quickly averted his gaze until DeHavillend straightened. At work, the man was unreadable, but here in his own home, he was clearly a doting husband.

"What has got you smirking like that?" he asked.

"Me?" Bennet tried to feign innocence.

DeHavillend ignored him and crossed the room to a liquor service on a side table. "What will you have?"

"A whiskey. Thank you."

DeHavillend brought his wife a glass of sherry first before returning with two glasses of amber fluid, handing one to Bennet.

"Have you seen the paper today?" Bennet asked.

"It was filled with nonsense," Libby said, setting her glass down on a side table. "From what my husband described to me, it was not as grotesque a picture as they painted it to be."

"Typical. I did not waste my time on it," DeHavillend put in.

"What baffles me the most is how there doesn't seem to be any kind of mot..." Bennet's voice trailed off as he turned his head toward the drawing room entrance and caught sight of Mary. When her eyes met his, he forgot to breathe.

She was, quite simply, beautiful.

"There's our Sherlock!" Libby smiled broadly.

Mary's eyes narrowed at her sister. "If that had come from Henry, I'd know what he means, but coming from you, I'm uncertain."

Libby flashed Mary a mischievous grin and she returned it with an even more mischievous one.

"Don't try to understand that interaction," DeHavillend murmured to Bennet. "You'll just get lost."

"This is something you're accustomed to, I suppose."

He nodded, finishing his drink.

"Bennet." Mary finally acknowledged him, and he bowed.

"Your Highness."

Her laugh was soft and sweet. "Oh no, you don't get to start that nonsense again."

He opened his mouth to say something in return, but the butler arriving to announce dinner prevented him. Probably a good thing. His head still felt muddled just from looking at her.

"I see the two of you are getting along. That is good." DeHavillend and his wife led the way in to dinner.

Bennet held out his arm for Mary. After some hesitation, she took it. This close, he noticed a shadow on her chin. A shadow that some work had clearly been put into to conceal. He suspected what it was, but decided to say nothing for now. She wouldn't have covered it if she wanted the bruise noticed. But he was immensely curious as to how she'd gotten it, shopping for lace.

"We have settled our differences, haven't we, Bennet?" she said.

"Yes, it appears that we have."

"You have to, for the good of the nation." Libby sat down to her husband's right, while Mary sat on his left. Bennet sat beside Mary. "We don't want the next thing the papers report to be headlined, *Detective Wars*." The baroness finished with a theatrical gesture.

DeHavillend laughed heartily and Mary leaned close to Bennet and whispered. "Observe the infamous Viscount Detective DeHavillend, in his natural habitat."

"Oh, I got a glimpse earlier."

She laughed and straightened as the first course was served: a deliciously creamy-looking corn soup.

"So, Sherlock and Brown," DeHavillend began.

"You too, Henry?" Mary let out a lady-like groan.

"Why not?" He shrugged. "As I was about to ask, tell me what strategy you've formed."

Bennet cleared his throat. "We decided to take each task together instead of assigning different roles. It was Mary's idea, and although I was skeptical about it at first, our trip to the athletics club to interview some of the people on our list changed my mind. It went a lot more smoothly due to Mary's presence."

Mary shot him a surprised look that morphed into a quick grin. They might not always agree, but they were in a good place now. And she was so confoundingly beautiful.

"That's a very good start. And what have you gathered today?"

"I thought Bennet gave you a report?" Mary teased.

"Nice try, young lady. I have not had time to read it yet."

"Not much, to be honest," she answered Henry. "It's puzzling how no one can point at who did this or why. I know her family adores her, and so do her friends and acquaintances. There doesn't seem to be any motive. Is it possible it could have been a random attack? That she just happened to be in the wrong place at the wrong time, when a madman snuck in through the window? I mean, that sounds far-fetched, but there is not even the whisper of anything negative in relation to Gertrude Fox."

"It's possible," Bennet said. "Though most unlikely. I wondered about the co-founders of the athletics club," Bennet said. "Lady Belmont in particular, given she found the body."

"And have you explored that and questioned Lady Belmont?" Henry asked.

"Not yet."

DeHavillend nodded sagely. "Do it. Plus, Gertrude's family, too."

The rest of dinner passed pleasantly, without talk

of murder, and Bennet could not recall the last time he had enjoyed a dinner like this. The small party moved to the drawing room afterward, before Mary and Bennet subsequently moved to the library.

"My collection, as promised," she said as she led him to a corner set of shelves. "This is one of my favorites." She picked up a small round gold clock covered in intricate scrollwork.

"This is a baroque piece, isn't it?"

"Indeed. It's the most ornamental piece in my collection but that's not why I like it."

"Why do you like it?" He moved closer to her, torn between continuing to watch her, and looking at the clock. Wisps of her hair had fallen from the loose knot atop her head, giving her a very sweet yet provoking look.

"It's also a music box." Mary turned it in her hand and wound the short lever. A tune began to play.

"This is an impressive piece, Mary."

"It is." Her eyes shone with pride. She picked up another, a small cottage with the face of the clock serving as the only window. "This one is Georgian. I found it on one of my adventures around town. It was thrown away."

Bennet noticed hinges on the cottage door, as well as tiny tracks. He took the piece from her and changed the time to a minute to the hour and waited. She gave him a look and smiled.

"What?" he asked.

"I'm glad you don't find this...odd."

"I would never think of you collecting rare clocks and fixing them up an odd venture. I think it is…fascinating."

The clock in his hand chimed and the cottage door opened. A woodcutter and his wife slid out along the tracks and turned in a little circle before retreating inside.

"I remember having something like this as a child. Only the figurines danced." A wistful smile came to his face.

"Is your family in Boston?" she asked quietly.

Bennet cleared his throat. "My mother lives here. She is the only family I have." He omitted the detail about how he rarely saw his mother.

Being pushed away by his mother, after his father's passing fourteen years ago, still pained him. He'd done everything he could to help alleviate her melancholy, to no avail.

His mother was the reason he had taken to studying psychology books, and his father's death the reason he decided to become a detective.

A small hand rested on his arm. Bennet blinked Mary into focus, scowling slightly.

"You looked a bit lost for a moment there."

"Memories. Not good ones."

She nodded, clearly understanding he did not want to talk about it. Perhaps he'd tell her the truth about himself one day. Just, not today.

He eyed the clock on the fireplace mantle and set the time he'd altered on the clock in his hand back to the correct time, before replacing it on the shelf.

"I think I should call it a night," he said. "Mary, I had a good time this evening. I enjoyed seeing your collection. And I have to confess, I also enjoyed seeing our favorite detective fawn over his wife."

She made a show of pouting. "That was the best part?"

He took her hand and raised it to his lips without thinking. Against her soft skin, he said, "I think you already know what the best part was, for me. I hope it may have been the same, for you?"

She flushed and gave an enigmatic smile. "Perhaps."

CHAPTER NINE

*M*ary watched Bennet walk out into the night and Bender close the door behind him. A soft sigh escaped her. Her hand went up to the pearl necklace around her neck and she toyed with it as she moved up the stairs, replaying the events of the evening in her mind. Bennet had won her over tonight.

The way he had admitted to Henry that she had actually been of value at the interviews today, had softened her. He had been honest and open about changing his mind about working with her. After dinner, that brief flash of vulnerability that had passed over his features at the mention of his family brought out a yearning in her. She wanted to know him better. She sensed he had a complex story to tell, and she wanted to know what it was.

Libby's voice as she played with Amelia rang

through the hallway, and Mary poked her head back in to the drawing room.

"I thought you would have retired already, Libby." Then she gazed at Amelia. "Look who's still awake at this hour." She held out her arms to take her niece, and the instant she did, Amelia began to snuggle and close her eyes.

She and Libby walked upstairs together to the nursery where Amelia's nanny, Eva, was waiting, a nervous look on her face. "How is she?" she asked.

"Ready to sleep." Libby reached for the baby. "She was quite irritable earlier," she explained to Mary. "I think she had a touch of colic."

"Oh, poor little one."

Libby handed Amelia over to the nanny, who tucked the baby into her crib. "She's well settled now. You have a magic touch with her, Mary!"

"Oh, well, thank you."

Libby suddenly asked, "So, do you mind telling me how you got that bruise?"

"A bru—" Mary sputtered. "Wha-what bruise?"

Libby gently tucked blankets in neatly around Amelia, before turning to face Mary with her hands on her hips. "You think no one saw it?"

"I thought Minnie covered it well."

"No amount of cosmetics can conceal that. It's darkening by the hour." Her eyes turned worried. "What happened, Mary?"

"Nothing serious."

"You will tell me what happened." She took Mary's arm and pulled her out of the baby's room.

"I started taking self-defense lessons today."

"Let me guess, you chose to take them in a part of town you're not supposed to travel to, alone."

"Maybe." She shrugged. "Oh, you know me so well, Libby." They walked down the hall to Mary's bedroom.

"Why didn't you ask Henry to coach you? He supports the idea of women learning to defend themselves."

"I wanted to do this by myself."

"And now you have a black chin to show for it."

"Well, at least it is not my eye. Oh, it's not that bad, surely. Henry or Bennet would have said something if it were." She went to the vanity table to peer in the mirror.

"Precisely why they said nothing."

The bruise was not looking good. Purple peeked through the layer of powder covering it. Mary let out a sigh. "Oh, well. What's done is done. The lesson itself was very helpful, I must say."

Libby sat down on the bed and released an exasperated chuckle. "Oh, Mary. You remind me of… well…me, a few years ago!" She brightened then. "So, Detective Brown. He seems like a nice man."

Mary smiled, knowing what her sister was hinting at. "Yes, he is."

"He's very handsome, too. Blue eyes, dark hair, tall and broad-shouldered…"

Mary picked up a small velvet pillow from the vanity table chair and threw it at her sister. "You're married, Libby!"

"Oh, happily so. I'm only pointing out young Bennet's positive attributes."

Mary rolled her eyes.

"And I noticed that you've not tried to crush him with your witty remarks as you do most gentlemen."

"Oh, believe me, Libby, I have. He is quite resilient."

"Oh!" She perked up. "That could make him the right man for you."

"Libby, I'm not seeking a suitor." She came to sit beside her sister on the bed.

"I know you're not. I was not looking for love when I found Henry, yet, here we are. Sometimes we find something special when we don't even know we're looking for it."

Her sister was right, but Mary's priorities varied from Libby's.

"If something happens, I might not sabotage it," she murmured.

Libby's eyes narrowed slightly and her lips curved up. "I believe you've just made a confession. Next time Penforth laments your lack of interest in marriage, I know what to tell him."

"You wouldn't." She shot Libby a warning look.

"Be nice and I'll take your secret to my grave."

Mary had had many potential suitors since her debut. She was only twenty and with a title and family wealth behind her, was considered an excellent prospect. Many in society could not understand why she would not accept a marriage proposal and take her proper place as a wife and eventual mother.

Mary mentally rolled her eyes at them all. Society should prepare, for she had many surprises in store for them.

"Fine."

"Back to Bennet Brown," Libby continued. "What do you think of him?"

"He is interesting," Mary admitted. "The most interesting man I've ever met. And he has a story."

"Oh? Do tell!"

"I don't know the story yet. I don't know a lot about him but I can tell he's a good man."

Her sister wiggled her fine brows suggestively. "And you do love a mystery."

"I most certainly do."

November 22, 1895

PREDICTABLY, MARY WAS EVEN MORE SORE WHEN SHE woke up the next morning. It took all of her willpower to get out of bed and go for her usual Friday morning cycle with her friend Lillian.

Concealing her bruise would be ineffective so she left the house with a dark chin.

"My heavens! What happened to your face?" Lillian gasped, horrified when she saw her.

"A punching bag," Mary replied breezily. "It was quite the sparring partner, I tell you."

"Oh, no doubt!" Lillian tilted her head from side to side, looking at Mary's chin. "Can I touch it?"

Mary proffered her chin for her friend's examination. Lillian pressed a finger into it and she winced. "Ouch!"

"Oh, sorry, I didn't mean to hurt you. So, how and why did you wrestle with a punching bag?"

"I took self-defense lessons at Drysdale's Gym yesterday. I registered for six lessons."

Lillian raised her pale brows. "I've heard of them. They have been advertising a bit. I even considered it myself there, for a bit. But they are not in the best neighborhood, Mary. Of all the gyms in Boston, you had to go to that part of town?"

"They advertised well."

Lillian's head moved from side to side, the blonde curls framing her face bouncing with the movement. "You're impossible."

"I know, and these bikes won't ride themselves." She began to pedal down the street away from Lillian's house.

It took a few minutes for her friend to catch up. "Tell me about the case," Lillian begged, as they rode side by side. "I saw the paper yesterday and they said it was gruesome."

"The paper exaggerated. The wound that killed

Gertrude was on the back of her head. Her face only had the slightest bruise. Less than mine."

"Do you have any suspects?"

"Sadly, no."

"I'm not surprised. Gertrude was a darling. I can't even imagine someone wanting to hurt her, let alone kill her."

"That seems to be the consensus from everyone." Mary sighed. "If this turns out to be the toughest case of the year, then I'm glad I'm working on it."

Lillian glanced in her direction. "This could be that chance you've been looking for."

Mary grinned, her hand coming up to adjust her hat. "I think it might be."

"And your detective partner? You didn't say much about him in your note."

Mary had written to her friend and arranged someone to send around the note after Henry accepted her onto the investigation team. Lillian would know how much that had meant to Mary and she had wanted to share the exciting news.

"His name is Bennet Brown. He's quite interesting."

Her friend's face quickly turned impish. "Interesting as a person, or interesting to work with?"

"Both."

"Oh, my goodness! You like him?"

Mary pedaled faster. "I'll tell you if you can catch me."

They raced for a while, laughing, their cheeks

pinkening in the cold Fall breeze. They slowed down when they arrived at Boston Common.

"Maybe I like him," she said, climbing down from the bike and walking with it. Lillian did the same.

"This is a first, Mary."

"There's always a first, isn't there? He was annoying in the beginning but we seem to have resolved our issues."

"What were they?"

"He thinks his experience as a police officer and a detective trumps my education. But I think he respects me now. Or at least, he seems to be able to accept that I might have something to offer."

"That's a good thing. Do you think there's a chance he might court you?"

"I haven't thought about it." The lie caused heat to rise from her neck right up to her cheeks.

The park was busy as usual and she was tempted to mount her bike again, but her thighs and rear needed the break. Especially after yesterday's boxing session.

"Oh, look, isn't that the Raven and Lady Sarah?" Lillian pointed.

Mary stared ahead and saw the couple strolling toward them, accompanied by Sarah's younger sister, Lady Arabella. Sarah and her sister Libby were firm friends, though Mary hadn't seen the sought-after society modiste recently due to Sarah being with child and feeling poorly.

She must be feeling better, to be out and about

taking a stroll with her husband, Tamworth Arbusson. Well, Sarah more waddled than strolled, and appeared to be leaning quite heavily on the Raven's arm. Mary waved at them and wheeled her bicycle over to say hello.

"How nice to see you this morning," Sarah said, stopping in front of them. Tamworth acknowledged them with a nod and a tiny smile. Lady Arabella's wide grin echoed her sister's greeting.

"I hear you are one of the detectives investigating Mrs. Fox's murder," Tamworth said.

"I am indeed. It's turning out to be quite a big case."

She noticed Sarah's eyes on her chin and tried to ignore the curiosity.

"It is Gertrude Fox," Sarah said. "That's bound to cause a stir. Did you know her very well?"

"A little. She was lovely. Though our interactions only really related to the Boston Athletics Club for Women."

"That will make solving her case a little easier, will it not?" Tamworth gave his wife's hand a little pat.

"Hopefully it will." When Mary's eyes found Arabella's, the girl's attention was on her bruise.

Everyone saw it but no one would mention it. She decided to face it with honesty. "I'm taking self-defense classes, and I had a run-in yesterday with a punching bag," she said.

"Goodness!" Sarah's eyes widened, and

Tamworth raised a hand to cough. Had he just tried to hide a laugh?

Mary frowned at him, until Arabella's eyes lit up and diverted her attention. "That sounds wonderful. Perhaps I could—"

"We can discuss that at home," Sarah said firmly.

Mary hoped Arabella would win her sister over. The more women took charge of their own lives, the more society would learn that it was all right for them to do that.

"Lillian, how is your brother?" Sarah asked, as if to change the subject.

"Oh, he's recovered now. It was as if he never fell off that ladder in the ballroom, and his arm was never broken. Expect wedding invitations soon. Only, this time round, he and his fiancée will make sure Hector is not the one to try and fix the ballroom chandelier on his own."

"We look forward to the invitation." She looked up at Tamworth who didn't seem as eager about attending a wedding. "Don't we, darling?"

He mumbled something that sounded like he agreed and now it was Mary's turn to stifle a laugh. Everyone knew how much the Raven disliked Boston Brahmin gatherings. Everyone also knew that, if his wife wished it, he would attend whatever gathering she suggested.

"I might visit with Libby and Anna soon." Sarah looked down at her rounded midsection and grimaced. "If my condition permits me, that is. Lovely seeing you, Mary. Lillian."

Once the trio was out of earshot, Lillian giggled. "That was awkward. They kept looking at your chin."

"I just decided I would provide the explanation and be done with it. Though, I've grown rather weary of explaining how I got it."

"I don't blame you." Lillian climbed onto her bike and began to pedal. "Are you attending the Countess of Lynch's soirée tonight?"

"Err...no. I would rather sit that one out."

"Why? And why are you still walking?"

"Look at my face. An unflattering drawing of me will be on the front pages tomorrow if I attend. And, I'm not riding because my body aches."

Lillian sighed. "I shall miss you terribly. I can imagine how the night will go. I'll be standing on the fringes of the room with no one to talk to."

"That tactic to make me feel guilty has been overused, Lilly. Besides, we both know you'll be whirling around the dance floor all evening, fighting off the hordes."

"Fine. But who will save me from unwanted dances?"

"You'll do fine. You're more than capable of—"

Something flipped in her chest at the sudden sight of Bennet Brown. She felt her cheeks tightening with a smile that was almost a grimace. What was he doing here? It looked as if he was...interviewing that man he was talking to.

"Who is that?" Lillian asked. "Tell me that's not *the* Bennet Brown."

"It is."

"He's even more handsome than you described." Lillian sighed.

"I didn't describe him as handsome."

Her friend waved a hand dismissively. "You didn't need to."

Bennet was in conversation with a gentleman that she could not recognize because his hat covered a part of his face. Bennet was holding his small notebook and pencil.

"Should we go and meet him?"

"No, Lilly. I believe he may be working."

Lillian pursed her lips for a moment before saying, "He appears to take his work very seriously."

That caused Mary's head to turn sharply. "Are you saying he's doing better than me?"

Her friend's hands came up in a gesture of surrender. "Your words, Mary. Not mine."

The man Bennet was speaking to turned just then, and she realized it was Jonah Fox, Gertrude's brother-in-law. Bennet, too, turned in their direction. When he saw them, he started as if shocked. After a moment, he tipped his hat in greeting.

Something wound tight inside Mary. Annoyance. Annoyance directed at herself. Here she was, cycling with her friend as if it were an ordinary Friday morning, while Bennet was out interviewing people.

He was on the job, as she should have been, too. She should be working on the case.

"What is that guilty look I'm seeing?"

Mary breathed deep and released it slowly. "I should be working."

"Then go and join him."

"You won't mind my leaving you?"

"No, I have to return home soon anyway. We're going to *La Robe Doreé* to start on my dress for Hector's wedding."

Sarah's dress-making business, *La Robe Doreé*, was renowned among the Boston elite and even though she herself was not working there right now due to her confinement, appointments at the famous modiste establishment were not something to be cancelled at short notice.

Mary nodded distractedly. "I'll see you later, Lilly."

"Good luck!" her friend called after her.

Mary had the feeling she might need all the luck she could get.

CHAPTER TEN

"Thank you for your time today, Mr. Fox," Bennet said. "And once again, my condolences on your family's loss."

"I should thank you for your good work, Detective." The man tried to muster a smile but he was obviously still too stricken to do so. "My wife is by the pond. I should return to her."

"Yes, of course. Please extend my best wishes to her."

Mary appeared at his elbow then but she'd arrived too late, for Mr. Fox had already turned and begun to leave.

"Good morning, Mary."

"I missed it," she mumbled, more to herself. But she quickly recovered and stared up at him. "Good morning, Bennet. I didn't realize we'd be working this morning."

"I had a bit of time on my hands and decided to

reach out to the victim's family. They mentioned they were taking the air on a walk, so I decided to join them."

"And you didn't think to let me know?"

"I...well...no." He swallowed hard. "I'm not used to working with a partner."

She narrowed her eyes, but eventually seemed to accept what he had said.

"Right. And what did you discover?"

"Nothing, as usual. Mr. Fox only had praise for Gertrude and lamented her loss. His wife, Gertrude's sister, was too distraught to speak directly with me. It seems that our victim was practically a saint."

Mary stared off into the distance, frowning. "I hope we're not hitting a wall. It is far too early in the investigation for that."

"I've been thinking the same thing." He took note of her bicycle and smiled. She was certainly a very... athletic person. "You ride?"

"Yes. I was here with my friend Lillian. We cycle every Friday morning."

He looked around for the friend. "Where is she?"

"She left. So, what else can we do today, in relation to the investigation?"

"I took the liberty of contacting Lady Belmont's residence, but she is unwell and not up to a visit today."

Mary's gaze sharpened, and his heart sank. "I should have involved you in that, too, shouldn't I?"

She just raised a brow at him, clearly not very pleased. He found himself wanting to please her.

"I have scheduled time tomorrow morning for that interview. And I was definitely planning to tell you of that. It was the only time Lady Belmont would agree to see me...err...us."

"Tomorrow is fine. We will do what is necessary, Bennet, to find Gertrude's killer."

He nodded. "All right. Well, the visit to the coroner's office is not scheduled until this afternoon. If you are not comfortable with—"

"I will attend with you." Her voice was a little icy. "We are partners, are we not?"

"Of course. Then I will meet you there at half past two o'clock."

He went to move away but on impulse turned back to her. "Before then, walk with me? Please?"

"All right." Finally, she seemed to thaw. A tiny grin decorated her lips. "Who knows, we might even find someone to interview."

They began to stroll down toward the pond. Bennet shoved his hands into his pockets as a means to keep himself from offering his arm to her.

She was quiet and contemplative today, like she had a lot on her mind. And the bruise he'd spotted last night had darkened. How had she gotten that?

"Mary—"

"I'm sorry but I have changed my mind. I have to go," she said abruptly. "I am not sure I will be joining you at the medical office after all. There's something I need to do."

"What do you mean?"

She climbed onto her bicycle and rode off without answering his question.

Bennet sighed and took off his hat and smoothed his dark hair. Her behavior just now seemed very strange, and that bruise she'd refused to explain worried him.

Had she gotten into a fight with someone?

He briefly contemplated running after her but he'd never catch up to her, not at the speed she was travelling on the bicycle.

BENNET TARRIED A LITTLE OUTSIDE THE CORONER'S office, hoping Mary would appear but it seemed she was, indeed, not going to attend after all. There seemed to be close to no activity in the office today, but an exception had been made for their case since the victim was so high-profile. He identified himself at the front desk before proceeding through to Mr. Burris's office.

"Good day, Detective," the coroner greeted when Bennet entered. "You're on time. Good."

"The results are ready, then?"

Burris slid a slim folder across his desk. Bennet opened it and pulled out the sheets inside, though he felt unaccountably guilty doing so without Mary by his side.

"We know the cause of death then. It is as suspected," he said after a moment scanning the contents of the pages.

"Yes, and the angle of the wound indicates that the attacker struck from above. Either they are taller than the victim, or were standing on elevated ground."

"It happened in a women's gym locker room. The former is more probable, I would suggest."

"Would you like to view the body?" Mr. Burris asked, and Bennet shook his head.

"I probably won't understand what I'm seeing. There's no need." He replaced the autopsy report in the folder and stood. "Thank you, Mr. Burris. I'll take my leave now."

"Good luck with the case," the man said genially.

Bennet was distracted as he left, thinking of the case and wondering where Mary had rushed off to, when someone bumped into his shoulder. A man.

"Pardon me!" he said.

"Watch where you're going," the other man hissed. He had a cigarette in his mouth and his greasy hair caught the light in the hallway of the medical building. There was a derby hat in one hand.

Something about him struck Bennet as odd. He was the sort of man one might typically see betting at a prizefighting event instead of at the medical office.

He watched the man continue down the hall

toward Mr. Burris's office. When he disappeared out of sight, Bennet shrugged and left.

His next destination was the DeHavillend Investigation Services Office where he attached the autopsy report to the Fox case file. When he stepped back out into the street, he could not get that strange man out of his thoughts. Instinct told him to return to the coroner's office to find out more.

Bennet hailed the first empty carriage he saw and returned to Mr. Burris's office, where he found the coroner preparing to leave.

"Detective...did you forget something?"

"Not exactly." Bennet closed the door behind him. "I saw a man come in on my way out. Bumped into him, in fact. He had an unlit cigarette in his mouth. Greasy hair and a brown coat, and carrying a derby."

"Ah, yes, I remember him." Mr. Burris's frown deepened. "He came in here as if he was looking for someone, and then said he'd lost his way and that this was the wrong office." Burris scratched his balding head. "Now that I recall, he seemed very odd. I didn't think to question him because he could have come to see our administrator, Mr. Ingram."

"I thought he seemed odd, too. How long ago did he leave?"

"Just after you. I don't know if he's still in the building."

Bennet thought for a moment, then his eyes widened as realization dawned. "That man didn't lose his way. He was looking for something."

"What?"

"That is what we're going to find out. Lead me to Gertrude Fox's body please, Mr. Burris."

The examiner stared at him. "You think there is a connection?"

"How many other cases are you dealing with right now?"

"Well, there are always cases, unfortunately, to keep us busy." He frowned. "But admittedly, none as high-profile as your current one."

"Precisely."

Mr. Burris picked up his keys and led Bennet down the hallway to the examination room. The stench of formaldehyde rose the closer they got, but Bennet tried not to let it bother him. What did perturb him, however, was the door they found unlocked.

"This can't be. I locked the door after finishing the report."

"Could Mr. Ingram have opened it?"

"No." He pushed the door and stepped inside. "Mr. Ingram is not a coroner nor a medical examiner. He is an administrator and has no access to the examination room without being accompanied by myself."

Bennet checked the lock for signs of forced entry. One tiny scratch indicated that the lock had likely been picked, and by someone who knew what they were doing, too. "Who else came in to work today?"

"Myself, Mr. Ingram, and the security guard,

Lambert, who would have signed you in at the front desk."

He approached the body on the examination table. "Lambert was not at his post when I left the building. The man may have entered without signing in."

"I think Lambert would have stopped him and questioned him." Burris was checking the body for signs of tampering.

"So it seems we may have a suspect," Bennet declared.

"Some progress." Mr. Burris looked up. "The body is intact."

"That's a relief. I'm going to return to the police station to update them, and see if I can work with an artist to get a likeness of the man drawn up. I'll question Lambert on my way out. Thank you, Mr. Burris."

"God speed, son."

Bennet strode to the front office, his steps determined and triumphant. He'd not expected to find a suspect this soon, not with how clueless they'd all been earlier. And he'd had a decent look at the man's face. He would not forget that one in a hurry.

Lambert was back behind his desk. "Nice day, Detective?"

"No, Lambert, a man snuck past you into this place earlier. He gained entry into the examination room."

Lambert's freckled face blanched. "I...I don't...I mean, I had to excuse myself for some minutes."

"How long were you gone?"

"About ten minutes, Detective."

"Well, that was enough time for someone to sneak in and out, it seems. You need to be more vigilant, Lambert."

"Of course, Detective. I simply had to go." His cheeks were bright with embarrassment.

"I understand."

"Will I be censured?" Lambert asked.

Bennet shrugged. "Best speak to Mr. Burris and explain," he advised.

A quarter of an hour later, Bennet was back at the DeHavillend Investigation Services Office, retrieving the case folder from the evidence locker. His eyes widened when he saw the addition in the locker.

"Holy God!" He laughed to himself. "This explains her haste earlier. She had a mission."

In one container was cigarette tobacco, and in another were strands of lank, greasy-looking hair. The new evidence matched the suspect he'd just seen. Coincidence or not, it appeared that he and Mary had both made progress...independently of each other.

CHAPTER ELEVEN

"You're not going to the Lynch ball?" Libby asked, rising from the drawing room sofa and crossing the room to snare a small cake from the plate that had been left on the sideboard.

"I'm tired," Mary replied, staring into the flames in the hearth. It was true. She had cycled straight from the park, all the way back to the athletics club, and spent quite some time crawling around in the dirt outside the window of the locker room where Gertrude was killed, before heading inside to check the scene of the crime. Not only had she found the door unlocked—which Martha most certainly would not have done—she had found the small pile of cigarette ash on the sill. Just as she was about to leave, she had seen the strands of long hair caught on the edge of the window frame.

She didn't think they'd been there earlier, or the

police would have seen them. Which meant someone had been lurking around since then, and had broken in to the crime scene. She had collected the samples as possible evidence, and then cycled to the office to store them before heading home.

All in all, she was ready to retire early to her room.

"You? Tired of a social event?" Libby laughed. "Don't tell me you're afraid of people seeing your bruise."

Mary had to admit that had a little to do with it, as well, but she truly lacked the spirit to attend a social gathering this evening. "Maybe."

"That's a pity. You might miss out on gathering valuable information. I hear that two ladies from Gertrude's circle will be in attendance. Notably, Lady Rochester and Mrs. De Claire."

"Really?" Mary shot to her feet. "All right. I'll go."

Libby shook her head. "Tsk! The things you'll do to solve this case."

"Your husband has done worse." Mary brushed past her, winking. "And as if you didn't know your information would change my mind!"

She called for Minnie and went upstairs to dress, choosing an elaborate pale green silk that flattered her creamy skin and dark hair. The dress sported both a long train and a lower neckline than her usual attire.

"We don't need to cover the bruise, Minnie."

"Really, Miss?"

"Yes. I'll have to make the bruise invisible by using

my charm. And this dress is pretty enough to aid me in that, don't you think? Besides, we can't cover it completely. Not without making me look like a clown."

"You're right, my lady." Minnie put away the cosmetics and got to work on Mary's hair. She pinned some tiny wax roses into her hair, circling the knot on top. A few wisps fell artfully to frame her face.

Mary smiled at her reflection. She'd have to depend on her wit and charm to carry her through this night, and she knew she could do it. It'd be easy to draw Lady Rochester and Mrs. De Claire into a conversation. They were very curious women and would readily talk about the murder of their friend.

"You didn't try to cover the bruise this evening?" Henry asked on the ride to the Lynch residence.

Mary turned from the carriage window. "No, I didn't. I don't see the need."

"Why did you cover it yesterday, then?"

Her shoulder lifted in a slight shrug. "I was younger and not as wise as I am today."

He smiled, before Libby drew his attention away with talk about one of their friends. Mary wanted to tell him about her discovery at the athletics club earlier, but she supposed now was not the time. It was not much, but she was proud that she had at least made some progress.

"Here we are!" Libby declared as the carriage rolled to a stop in front of the grand home.

When Mary was assisted down, she observed how

many carriages were queuing and a grin broke out on her face. A lot of people to watch; a lot of people with whom to discuss the murder. As they joined the guests entering the ballroom, she whispered to Henry.

"Don't worry if you don't see me for some time. I'll be in the crowd talking with some of the people on our list."

He nodded. "I trust you can take care of yourself."

Once inside, she spotted Lillian dancing with a gentleman and gave her friend a tiny wave. She weaved her way through the mingling guests, making good progress until a hand grabbed her elbow and pulled her to a stop. She turned to see Oliver Blackwood, a suitor she'd turned down precisely twelve months past. Pasting on a stiff smile and tuning her voice to sound pleasant, she said, "Mr. Blackwood, what a pleasant surprise."

"Indeed, Your Highness. I did not expect to see you here this evening."

"Yes, well…here I am." Her gaze travelled slowly around, seeking a savior from what could become an awkward situation. When none was forthcoming, she decided to save herself. "Please excuse me, there is somewhere I need to be."

"This is how you greet an old friend?" His words came out through clenched teeth and she took a retreating step. One of the reasons she'd rejected his suit was because of his mercurial temper and fondness for too much whiskey.

"We were never friends, Mr. Blackwood. Please excuse me." She gathered her skirts and moved away from him as quickly as she could.

The matrons occupied chairs along the left wall of the ballroom and she caught sight of Lady Rochester in one of the chairs, fanning herself vigorously. Mary approached her, wearing her brightest smile.

"Lady Rochester."

The woman looked up. "Your Highness, whatever are you doing over here in the older ladies' side of the room? You should be dancing."

"Oh, I was looking for my mother. I just arrived with my sister and the Viscount."

"I've not seen dear Christiana, I'm afraid." She squinted at Mary. "What do you have there on your chin?"

Lady Rochester was in her late sixties and well past the point of caring about propriety. When most people would have avoided acknowledging her bruise, Lady Rochester had no hesitation in pointing it out.

Mary sighed dramatically. "Oh, it's a long story, Lady Rochester."

"I have time, child." She patted the cushion of the chair beside her. "And since you are not dancing, sit down and tell me."

This was working better than she'd anticipated. She sat and turned to face the matron. "I was doing something unconventional."

"Oh?" Her jaded blue eyes brightened and she leaned forward. "Was it scandalous?"

"On some level, you could say so..." She deliberately trailed off to further pique the older lady's interest.

"Tell me more, child," she prodded, seemingly impatient.

"Well, I was boxing."

Lady Rochester's eyes sparkled. "How interesting! With a man or a woman?"

Mary lowered her lashes as though she was ashamed. "It was a punching bag."

Lady Rochester guffawed, drawing the curious gazes of nearby guests. "Oh, you funny girl! You have just brightened my evening. That is an excellent joke, Princess Mary."

"Oh, but it is not a joke. I punched the thing and then got distracted. It came back and hit me. Knocked me right on my..."

She pointed to her rear, and Lady Rochester laughed more. "That is even funnier!" When she calmed down, she said, "I miss the days when I could sport effortlessly. The most I can do now is a gentle stroll through the park. Enjoy your youth, girl."

Mary's grin was wide. "Oh, I do, Lady Rochester."

"And hone your fighting skills. Look what happened to poor Gertrude." The matron's face fell. "Such a terrible, terrible loss. She could not defend herself from that perfidious soul."

"It is very tragic. I know you were her friend, and

I am so very sorry. Do you know who could have done it?"

"There are a thousand speculations out there, yet none seem right." She shook her silver head. "I truly don't know, child."

"I'm sorry, Lady Rochester. When did you last see Gertrude?"

"We had tea together the day before she died. She was talking about what she would do to improve the athletics club to attract more young women like you."

"I hope someone fulfills that dream for her." Mary placed her hand on Lady Rochester's, genuine in her words. Gertrude had done so much for the advancement of women in sport. It would be very sad to see it all end now.

"I hope so, too, my dear." Lady Rochester clutched her hand. "And thank you for sitting and entertaining me for a while."

"You're welcome, my lady."

"Now, run along and find your peers. Sitting here with an old lady will not do well for your marriage prospects."

Mary laughed at that and rose to her feet, deciding to take a break in the ladies' retiring room for a few minutes.

A calm feeling came over her the minute she exited the ballroom. She loved attending society events, but sometimes she appreciated the quiet, too. Like today. Her jeweled slippers clicked against the marbled floor of the quiet hallway as she tried to locate the ladies' retirement room.

"Running from the party already?" a deep and unwelcome voice rumbled.

Mary's heart sank. Mr. Blackwood had not taken her rebuff well, it would seem.

She drew in a deep breath and clenched her fists at her sides. "What do you want from me, Mr. Blackwood?"

"I thought you would have guessed that by now." He took a step toward her and she immediately retreated back.

"I don't have time for your silly guessing games. Goodbye." She turned to leave but his hand shot out and grabbed her arm in a rough grip.

"You are not going anywhere until I say so." His hold tightened and he yanked her to him.

"Unhand me, you fool!" She tried to wrest her arm from his firm grasp but he held on. "Let me go!"

"You made a fool of me once when you rejected me. I am not going to let you do it a second time."

Mary clenched her teeth and pulled her leg back, preparing to kick him just the way Mr. Drysdale had shown her with the punching bag.

"Step away from her!" A low menacing growl swept down the hall.

A gasp escaped her lips. "Bennet?" she whispered. What was he doing here?

Mr. Blackwood immediately released her and stepped away. "Who the hell are you?"

"Someone you do not want to cross. I am Detective Brown and I can make things very difficult for you."

"I...you..." Mr. Blackwood sputtered, then seemed to think twice before stomping past Bennet.

But Bennet was not ready to let him go just yet. He grabbed Blackwood's collar and yanked him back, sending him stumbling. Mary quickly stepped out of the way.

"Apologize," he commanded, rage hardening every angle of his sculpted face. "Apologize to the princess. Now."

Blackwood huffed before mumbling something.

"What was that?"

"I beg your pardon, Your Highness," he grated out.

"Now, disappear from here."

When Blackwood scurried away, Bennet released a breath and stepped toward her. He was obviously still enraged but he managed a tight smile. "Are you all right, Mary?" He took her hands.

"Are you trying to be the knight who saves the princess?" she said, in an attempt to lighten the atmosphere.

"You didn't need rescuing. It looked to me as if you were about to deal him a decent blow."

"Why did you interrupt me then?"

"I got angry. I hate it when a man thinks he can overpower a woman. I had to do something." His thumbs stroked the backs of her hands and her eyes fluttered shut for a moment, enjoying the sensation. "How did you get that bruise?" His voice was calmer now.

She opened her eyes again. "I visited Drysdale's Gym yesterday when I left you. I registered for their self-defense lessons after a punching bag did this to me."

Relief passed over his features. What had he been thinking? Had he been concerned that she may have been attacked? "You signed up because the punching bag hit you?"

"No, I had a trial lesson, during which the punching bag hit me and that was only because I got distracted by someone yelling. I registered after that."

"So you were not shopping for lace." His eyes pierced hers. "You little imp."

Calling her a little imp only made her laugh. "I need to learn to defend myself. You saw what happened just now."

"Yes, you're right. But you don't need to go back to Drysdale's Gym. I've seen that one advertised, and it is too far away and not in a good location for ladies such as yourself. I could train you."

"After what you said yesterday at lunch?"

"Was it only yesterday? Seems longer ago than that. And I take my words back. You do need to be able to defend yourself."

"And you think I will allow you to train me?" she asked archly.

"I'm the best option you have. The weather is

cooling by the day and I don't suppose traveling across town in a streetcar in the middle of winter is a lot of fun."

"*That* is your argument, Detective?"

"Oh, I have more, Your Highness." His grin was contagious. "There is a gym at the office." He held up a silencing finger when she opened her mouth to argue. "And DeHavillend will take you more seriously if you train here under his nose."

Mary scoffed. "Henry knows I went to Drysdale's Gym. His wife told him."

"My points are still valid," he insisted.

"I shall think about it."

"Good."

She was reminded, then, of her surprise in seeing him at the ball. "What on earth are you doing here, anyway?" she asked, taking in his appearance. He was dressed in an immaculate black tailcoat with a crisp white bowtie and a pleated dress shirt. His dark hair was neatly coiffed and slicked back in a style that showed off his handsome face to perfection.

"I believe I'm attending an event that the Countess of Lynch invited me to."

Her eyes widened at that. "I didn't…" She left the statement unfinished. No matter how she phrased it, her words would not sound kind.

"You didn't think I was a part of your world?" he asked, his tone soft and teasing.

"You seemed…different to those I've always known."

A grin appeared on his face then. "Maybe I am."

"I'll be more mindful of my assumptions from now on."

Bennet tucked her hand into the crook of his elbow. "Shall we dance? I believe we have a case to discuss."

"Yes, Detective, we do. And yes, I do believe I would enjoy a dance."

"I met a surprise this afternoon in the evidence locker." He began to walk her back to the ballroom, keeping his voice low as he spoke to her.

"Yes, I'm sorry about earlier, but I had an epiphany at the park and ran off to check. I remembered reading that killers like to cover their tracks and to do so, they sometimes return to the crime scene. I thought there was a good chance of this one returning, especially since it is well-known the gym is currently closed. The odds of the person being seen is slim."

"So, you fled without taking me with you. I'm wounded, Mary." He clutched his chest but the smile tugging at the corners of his lips betrayed him.

She swatted his shoulder. "I had to confirm my theory first. You have a reputation when it comes to underestimating my education."

They reached the ballroom in time for a waltz and he steered her toward the dancefloor. "I'm learning," he said.

She looked up at him with bewilderment. "Is that humility coming from you?"

"Don't get accustomed to it." One of his hands came to rest on her waist and he pulled her to him.

Her eyes met his vivid blue ones, and his mouth slanted. A warm feeling washed over her as he tugged her closer but not enough to be considered inappropriate. It felt nice being in Bennet's arms. They moved with the music, little flutters forming in her stomach.

"You are very graceful," he murmured close to her ear. "You feel as if you're floating."

"I love dancing," she breathed, delighting in the moment: the music, the dance, being in his arms.

"What did you find when you returned to the gym?"

"Someone did return to the locker room, and they used the door. I found it unlocked and Martha would never leave that door unlocked while investigations are going on. The window was open a crack as well, and there were ashes on the sill."

"First, he leaves blood, and now ashes. This man is sloppy."

"Man?" Mary asked a little too loudly. Her eyes darted around to make sure she'd not drawn any unwanted attention from the dancers around them. She lowered her voice. "What do you mean *man*?"

"We have a suspect."

Her mouth dropped open before she snapped it shut.

"I saw a man at the coroner's office," Bennet explained. "He had dark greasy hair, a brown coat and a derby hat, and there was an unlit cigarette in his mouth."

"It could be the same person, but how did you know?"

"I just had a gut feeling that something about him was odd. He seemed out of place in the medical environment, and that got me suspicious. I returned to the coroner's office after attaching the autopsy report to the case folder and discovered that he had entered the building without leave. He picked the examination room lock *and* left the door open. He must have gone in to check the body."

Mary sucked in her lips. They had a suspect! Finally, they were getting somewhere in the case! She didn't care that Bennet had found the man. She had found a clue, too. Something that could connect the man Bennet had seen to the murder.

"Why do you think he wanted to check on the body?"

"I cannot say."

The dance came to an end and they parted. "I'll have a turn around the room with Lillian. My interviews are not over."

"I might do the same." He raised her hand to his lips and kissed her knuckles.

Lillian was in a conversation with one of the younger guests when Mary found her. "Mary, you're here!" She wrapped her in a hug. "I suffered three dances."

"But you survived, did you not?"

"Oh, stop it." She looped her arm through Mary's and they began to stroll around amongst the crowd of guests.

"Your bruise is visible, you know."

"Of course, I know. I am not concerned about it any longer. Sure, I will be talked about for a couple of days, but gossip always dies down eventually."

"True."

"Oh, there is Mrs. De Claire. I need to interview her."

Mrs. De Claire was surrounded by a group of ladies, making broaching the topic of the murder tricky. But she approached them anyway.

"I'm never visiting that gym again," one of the ladies was saying. "I am revoking my membership as soon as they re-open."

"So am I...before I end up getting murdered, too," another said.

"I don't think murder is enough reason to revoke your membership." Mary joined in the conversation. "It is beyond anyone's control, and besides, now the club will likely be even more vigilant about security than before."

"They should have protected us before. It is shameful."

"It's on Newbury Street, in a lovely location, well-protected. This was a one-off, I'm sure."

"I don't believe that." The woman sniffed and turned her face away.

"What we should be wondering about is who did it, and why." Mary declared.

Every lady in the group turned to look at her.

"Do *you* know who did it, Your Highness?" Mrs. De Claire, who had said nothing until now, piped up.

"Not yet. I find it curious that no one can think of any reason whatsoever to have harmed poor Gertrude Fox."

Mrs. De Claire was quiet for a moment before she said, "Gertrude didn't have enemies. She was lovely."

"Yet still someone robbed her of her life," Mary returned. She decided to leave the group as there was nothing more for her to gain, but not without a parting statement. "Gertrude put a lot of work into establishing a place where women could train and enjoy sporting activity, and have a good time, without censure. It would be most unfortunate if she lost members because of the circumstances of her death. Where is your sense of solidarity and support?"

Some of the ladies stared at her as though she'd sprouted a new head, but a couple of them began to nod and look thoughtful. Mrs. De Claire smiled at her, as if she approved. They gave each other a small nod, and then Mary turned on her heel and left.

"That was very bold, Mary, even for you," Lillian said.

"Well, I am bolder now."

"Since last week?" Lillian playfully poked her finger into Mary's arm. "Don't get cocky!"

"I am investigating a murder, Lillian. I have to look and sound the part."

"Who would you like to interview next?"

Her eyes scanned the room, landing on Bennet. He was talking to a young woman, Rowena Lincoln. She was a distant cousin of Gertrude Fox's late husband. Mary tilted her head as she watched them. A moment later, he escorted the young lady to the dancefloor.

"Good move, Detective," she murmured, her lips curling up.

Several conversations later, Mary was worn out. She'd gained nothing valuable from any conversation. Nothing! All everyone did was speculate and steal glances at her chin—although that did not bother her half as much as the gossip.

She was shifting her weight from one foot to another, wondering if she could leave, when she felt a tap on her shoulder. She turned to see Lady Westwood. "I didn't realize you were acquainted with Lord Cannington," Lady Westwood said.

"Who?" She blinked confusedly.

"The Earl of Cannington," she repeated.

Mary followed the line of the woman's gaze, seeing Bennet talking to an older man she had never seen before. She frowned. "I'm afraid I'm not ac—"

She stopped mid-sentence as the realization hit her like a ton of bricks.

CHAPTER TWELVE

"Oh, we…yes, we're good friends…yes." Her stomach tumbled in knots when the truth settled. "Please excuse me, my lady," she said through clenched teeth.

"Of course."

Mary wove her way through the crowd, her eyes on Bennet, her insides roiling with anger. How could he have kept this from her?

"My lord," she said sweetly, tapping his shoulder.

He turned around, his automatic smile freezing when he saw that it was her. "Mary?"

"Can I speak with you for a moment?"

He followed her out of the ballroom and once they were in the hallway, she caught his coat sleeve and dragged him into the first room she could find. A library.

"Are you the Earl of Cannington?" she demanded.

"I don't know what you're talking about." He wrenched his arm free of her grasp.

"Don't play with me, Bennet. Are you, or are you not, the earl?"

He shrugged. "So, what if I am?"

"So what?" Mary was taken aback by his apparent lack of concern about her feelings. "You lied to me."

"I did not! I may have omitted the truth but I did not lie." He stalked toward a window and raked his fingers through his hair before turning back to look at her.

"What is the difference?"

"There is a difference," he insisted. "I have not hidden anything. You could have asked anyone you wanted and they would have told you who I am. There is no need for you to be angry because I happen to have a title."

"It isn't that, and you know it. Bennet, we work together," she seethed. "We're partners. This is not something you *omit*."

He walked slowly back toward her. "I didn't think it was important because I rarely use my title." He towered over her, his eyes flashing annoyance. "I don't have land, nor a lot of wealth or influence. Going around and making my status known to all and sundry doesn't serve any purpose except vanity."

But I'm not all and sundry, Mary thought. *At least, I didn't think I was.*

She looked down at her shod toes peeking out from beneath the gown, directing her anger at herself.

Here he was, ignoring his title while she reveled in hers. Every time she was introduced as Her Royal Highness, Princess Mary, she felt a rush of delight. Libby had chosen to shun that title for her lesser one, and people knew her as Baroness Esk in her own right, as well as a Viscount's wife now that she was married to Henry.

When Mary had made her debut, she decided to do the opposite of Libby, and embrace being a princess. Only, she wanted to be a modern princess. The woman who could have it all.

Was she being vain and stupid in her aspirations?

His attitude made her feel guilty. Her eyes snapped back to his, lots of different emotions roiling for dominance. She saw that his jaw was clenched tight and every cord in his neck was taut. Clearly, she was not the only one fighting a myriad of emotion.

Bennet took a step forward and she copied his movement. They were now merely a hairsbreadth apart. All he'd have to do was inch down a little and his lips would be on hers.

Mary's breath caught as the air between them sparked with anger and desire. Her body trembled and it took all she had to keep her hands clenched at her sides. If she dared allow them to move, she'd find herself either slapping him across the face or pulling him close and initiating a kiss. Neither option was proper behavior for a lady.

She refused to give in to either of those primitive

urges. She released her breath slowly, and managed to step away.

"Is there anything else you haven't disclosed, that you think I should know?" she asked.

"No."

She turned on her heels and left the room. In the hall, she spied Margaret Seaton coming out of the ballroom. Bennet made his exit then, and Mary saw Miss Seaton's eyes widen and her hand flutter up to her mouth.

Oh, dear!

Miss Seaton was one of society's biggest gossips. Mary hoped she would not jump to conclusions. More importantly, she hoped the woman would keep her mouth shut.

HE WAS MORE UPSET THAN HE EXPECTED, ABOUT Mary's reaction to discovering his title. Why it bothered him so much, he did not wish to question. Regardless, Bennet chose not to return to the ballroom. Instead, he made his way to the front entrance and stopped there, watching from the shadows as Mary was assisted into the DeHavillend family carriage and disappeared down the grand driveway.

He turned and made his way down the hall. He would have to find the hostess and bid her farewell. It was time to get away from the cloying atmosphere of high society's clutches.

He hadn't lied to Mary. An omission was not a lie. He hadn't even considered that she might be angry— perhaps hurt—that he hadn't been forthcoming with the whole truth. Frankly, he'd not thought it important, or that there might be consequences.

He didn't like this feeling at all. He didn't like being angry with her or having her angry with him in return. He didn't like the fact that he had obviously hurt her feelings.

Bennet realized he should not be angry with her for reacting as she had. They needed to trust each other in order to successfully work together. Keeping his identity hidden had put that trust at risk. He saw now that he had made an error.

"Lord Cannington? Bennet, dear. Surely you are not leaving just yet?" It was the Countess of Lynch, his mother's cousin. She grabbed his elbow and held tight.

"Something has come up, I'm afraid, and I have to leave immediately."

"Is it your mother?" Her eyes shone with concern.

"No, my mother is quite well. This is in regards to a police matter."

She didn't know that he'd not seen his mother in almost a year, though he still heard how she was faring, through mutual friends and acquaintances.

"Oh, you and your police work! I'll let you go then." The countess released his arm. "It was lovely to see you here, Bennet. Please come out to these events more often. One would think you're not one of us. I hear you sometimes even travel about town without your carriage."

His brows shot up. "My lack of use of my carriage is what concerns you?"

"Well." She waved a hand aimlessly. "I'm just advising you to act according to your station in life."

He was proud of himself for not rolling his eyes in front of her. "Good night, cousin."

He retrieved his greatcoat and hat from the coat room before stepping out into the night. He was tempted to walk home, just to spite the countess, but he was not in the mood to be back in his bachelor lodgings just yet. So, he called for his carriage and rode to the Barbican, one of the most exclusive gentlemen's clubs in Boston.

It was owned by Tamworth Arbusson, also known as the Raven. In the past, the Raven had had a dark and mysterious reputation, but now, under the guiding light of his wife, Lady Sarah, it was said that the Raven had begun to move out of the shadows.

During the ride, all Bennet could think of was Mary and how this might affect their work. They'd made some progress, at least, but they were nowhere near concluded.

When his carriage stopped in front of the club he alighted quickly. He rarely visited gentlemen's clubs, but this one was his first choice when he did so. He was admitted in and shown to a private booth.

Immediately, an acquaintance, George Meyer, approached him.

"Brown!" He clapped him on the back. "What brings you here?"

Bennet leaned back in his chair. "The need of a good drink."

"And some company?"

He released a long breath. "I wouldn't mind the company. Join me."

Meyer sat in the chair opposite as a waiter set down a snifter beside Bennet and poured him a few fingers of brandy.

"What has you in such a dour mood, my friend?" To the waiter, Meyer said, "Bring me one of those, too."

Bennet only shook his head, disinclined to talk.

"I heard you're the investigator on the Fox case. How is that going?"

"I am one half of the investigation team," he corrected. "And not as well as I'd hoped. Normally, when it comes to murder, there will be some whiff of scandal, or something…" He released an exasperated sigh. "There is nothing. The woman was practically a saint! Have you heard anything, Meyer?"

"Nothing. This case is indeed a silent one."

Bennet sipped his drink slowly, thinking of their suspect. "Have you ever come across a man with dark greasy hair, and who often walks around with an unlit cigarette hanging out of his mouth? He was carrying a derby hat, if that makes any difference."

The description was general, he knew. It could be anyone.

Meyer leaned back, swirling his drink in his hand. "The underground, members of the Mafia, like to wear derbys, I believe. But that is of no import to your case. We all know what kind of woman Gertrude was. She would not have been involved in anything related to the Mafia."

"You're right." Bennet could not think of any reason for a criminal organization's involvement in Gertrude's death. But, as a detective, he could not rule anything as impossible.

His thoughts changed direction. He needed to speak with someone about this. *Mary.* She had such an astute mind, and a different way of looking at things. Surely, together, they could come up with a plan of action?

Then his heart sank as he remembered what had transpired earlier. He didn't think Mary would want to speak to him again tonight.

That left no other option than to find DeHavillend. He checked his pocket watch and realized his mentor would likely be well home from the ball by now.

He rose from his chair and reached out to shake Meyer's hand. "Talking with you has been very insightful, Meyer. Until we meet again."

"Leaving so soon?"

"Such is the life of a detective." With a brief nod, he left.

Bennet's mind was sharper as he climbed into his carriage. Before the door closed, his eyes swept his surroundings. Movement in the shadows caught his attention and his head snapped in that direction. A man stood near a street lamp just beyond the circle of light.

The first thing Bennet made out was the derby hat on his head. Not uncommon, except that the man was staring straight at him, as if silently challenging him to a confrontation.

He reached into the side pocket in the carriage for the Colt revolver he always carried with him. Transferring it to his jacket pocket, he stepped down from the carriage and approached the man.

The closer Bennet got, the more it became clear that this was not the man from the medical examiner's office. This man was larger and taller. But they could be connected. Unexpectedly, the man turned and began to run.

Bennet chased him.

The man was remarkably fast for his size. Bennet considered himself fit, but still found it hard to catch up. The man skidded around a corner into an alley and Bennet followed, pulling out his Colt as he entered the dark space.

An eerie silence settled over him. He could hear nothing but the continued pounding of feet against the ground.

Bennet's lungs burned from the exertion and sweat beads formed on his brow.

Then the footfalls disappeared, and it was only the sound of his own labored breathing that assailed his ears. He stopped, doubling over and opening his mouth wide to draw in more air. His grip on his revolver tightened and he blinked in the darkness, able to see better now that his eyes had adjusted.

No one was in the alley with him. The man was gone. He had most likely entered one of the buildings on either side of the alley, using the darkness as his cloak. But which one? And why had he stood there, staring at Bennet in such a challenging way?

He cautiously backed out of the alley. He was determined to find Gertrude's killer, but was not foolish enough to remain in a dark alley by himself at midnight. Especially when it was possible that he may have been lured there on purpose.

He returned to his carriage and drove to the DeHavillend residence without further incident. It was well past midnight when he arrived.

The butler was visibly surprised to see him on the doorstep, but given Henry's detective business, he was likely used to visitors at strange hours.

"Is the Viscount in?" Bennet asked. "I wouldn't rouse him this late, except it is urgent."

"Yes, sir, he returned earlier with his family." He opened the door wider and stepped aside to let Bennet enter. "Follow me, please."

The butler showed him to the library before going to fetch DeHavillend. He crossed the room to Mary's clock collection, the memories of their time together that evening drawing a smile out of him. That evening, she awoke a yearning in him.

A yearning to share something of himself with her.

"Brown, is everything all right?" came DeHavillend's voice.

"It's about the case. I may have found a lead and it couldn't wait until morning. I hope that is fine with you?"

"Of course, it is fine. There is a killer on the loose and as long as they are out there, innocent lives are in danger. You can come at any time of the day or night."

Bennet nodded and strode to one of the chairs in front of the lit fireplace. DeHavillend was lowering himself into one when he paused.

"Mary is unlikely to be asleep yet; perhaps she should join us?"

Bennet considered it. She had been so upset with him earlier. "Maybe we should let her sleep and catch her up in the morning."

DeHavillend raised his brows in question. "Are you sure?"

"Err…yes. I guess…yes. I am."

His mentor's eyes narrowed for a short stint but eventually he nodded and sat down.

"As you know from the report, we now have a suspect," Bennet began. "I dropped in to the Barbican this evening, and spoke with George Meyer. He mentioned that the members of some crime organizations are known to wear derby hats."

Bennet rose from his chair and moved about. Moving helped him think.

"What if this is tied to a criminal organization? To the entire world, Gertrude Fox is an angel with no enemies. What if she was not who we all thought she was?"

DeHavillend's head bobbed.

"The most intriguing thing happened after I left the club. There, on the street, was a man wearing a derby—not the one I saw at the coroner's office, however—and he looked like he knew who I was. I chased him into an alley where he disappeared. These two men could be connected to the murder."

"Did you get a good look at his face?"

Bennet's fingers raked his hair. "No, I did not. It was definitely not the same man as at the medical office, but I couldn't make out much more than shape and size."

"We can work with that. In the morning, you will meet with a sketch artist so we can have posters out on both the men you've seen." DeHavillend's gaze met his. "You did well by coming here immediately."

"Thank you, sir. The other thing I wanted to raise, was Lady Adele Belmont," he said. "She's been avoiding the public since the murder. She might know something that could help us, so Mary and I have arranged to visit her in the morning."

DeHavillend rose and walked over to the liquor service. "Drink?"

"No, thank you," Bennet declined. "I need to keep a clear head."

DeHavillend shrugged and poured a whiskey for himself. "Did something happen with Mary?"

A reluctant chuckle burst from Bennet. "Straight to the point, eh?"

"She is my wife's sister. And my employee."

"She found out this evening that I am the Earl of Cannington."

DeHavillend's brows came together. "Any particular reason why you kept that information from her?"

"Honestly, it never came up. I did not think it would be important at the time."

"Well, make sure you sort it out. Do not allow small squabbles to come between the two of you. It may affect your work."

"I will be mindful of that. Thank you." He straightened. "I will take my leave now."

"Until morning. There is still a lot to do."

a soft knock sounded at her door and Mary called for whoever it was to enter. The door opened and Libby slipped in.

"You're not asleep. Good."

"What is it?" she asked. She was alone and brushing her hair. Not wanting company, she'd dismissed Minnie once she was out of her corset.

"Henry wants to see you. It's about the case." Her sister came to stand behind her at the vanity table. "Detective Brown just left."

"He was here?"

"Yes. I think there have been some developments."

Mary stood and went to retrieve a heavy velvet robe. Wrapping herself in it, she followed Libby out of the room, wondering what was so serious that Bennet had to visit this late. And why was she not called to this meeting?

Then she asked herself a question. Would she have wanted to see him?

No, she would not. She was still upset, though with him, or herself, she wasn't sure.

They found Henry in the library. He didn't waste any time, quickly explaining how Bennet had chased a strange man into an alley only to have him disappear. The derby hat. And Gertrude's possible involvement with a criminal organization...

Mary sat down. "This case is turning more surreal every day."

"You can say that again," Henry said.

"Something I was thinking about, when Libby came to fetch me..."

"Yes?" her brother-in-law said.

"Is it worthwhile questioning Gertrude's lawyers and business partners? She supported a lot of charities and businesses, not just the athletics club. I was actually wondering if perhaps one or more of her sources of income might be questionable. Now that you've mentioned Bennet's experience tonight and the possible criminal connection...she couldn't have been killed by those kinds of men without some sort of involvement with them, surely?"

"That is an excellent idea, Mary. I believe you're right. Allebie and Anderson Law Firm is the legal team handling her affairs. I will arrange for you and Bennet to meet with them."

Mary studied him in silence for a moment. "Henry, why was I not called when Bennet arrived?"

Instead of answering her question directly, he said, "There appears to be some tension between you two."

"Ah." Mary stared down at her hands on her lap. She liked Bennet more than she'd ever liked any man, and his keeping secrets upset her much more than she would have liked. Feeling vulnerable was not something she enjoyed.

"We will talk about this in more detail in the morning. I believe you are interviewing Lady Belmont then."

Her heart sank. She had forgotten about that. "Would you mind sending a message to Bennet to let him know he can undertake that task without me? In the meantime, I will start looking into the law firm angle."

"I can do that," Henry said gently. "But you will need to sort it out with Bennet."

She nodded.

"Go and get some rest now," Henry said.

She stood. "Good night Henry. Libby."

Mary felt more drained than usual by the time she returned to her bed chamber. She could not afford to lose concentration now. The case was progressing and they might be done with it in a matter of days. Being professional was vital if she wanted to attain the credibility she craved. Allowing Bennet to distract her was not an option.

She would need to put aside her personal hurt, and try to get on with the job.

November 23, 1895

BENNET CLIMBED THE STEPS TO THE FRONT DOOR OF the home of Lady Belmont. It was only a few minutes past eight and normally far too early a time to be calling. But this was not a social call. And he was a detective.

Henry had sent the message from Mary, and passed on her idea about following up with Gertrude's legal team. A grand notion. She really was an asset to the team, though he had to confess to being a little nervous to see her again after what had transpired the previous evening.

He lifted the brass knocker and released it. The door opened immediately and a stocky butler looked at him from head to toe in a manner that made him feel as though he was the most insignificant creature in the world.

"I am Detective Bennet Brown," he announced. "I have arranged an audience with her ladyship."

The butler cleared his throat. "Her ladyship is still abed, and I believe she was expecting Her Royal Highness Princess Mary, but not at this hour."

"The princess is not attending today, and besides, we have waited long enough. Wake your mistress. This is about the murder of Mrs. Gertrude Fox, and I wish to speak with her now."

"Do come in." The butler was grudging, but at least he allowed Bennet to enter.

Bennet followed the man to a small salon where he was left alone for over twenty minutes. He kept himself busy studying a book about pirates that he found on one of the side tables. He was immersed in the story when Lady Belmont joined him. A lady's maid accompanied her, and stood in the corner of the room, awaiting instruction from her mistress.

"Good morning, Detective." Her voice was thin and dry.

Bennet got to his feet and bowed slightly. "Good morning, my lady."

"What is so important that you had to disturb my sleep this early on a Saturday morning? I have already spoken with the police about Gertrude's murder, and I was expecting yourself and Princess Mary, but at a later hour."

"The princess has been delayed elsewhere, and I have some questions of my own."

She lowered herself into a chair and looked up at him. "Sit and let us talk, then."

"You were in business with the victim. What can you tell me about Mrs. Fox's business conduct?"

"She was a practical woman, and very intelligent. She entrusted the management of her wealth to a good team."

"Is the athletics club the only establishment in which you were in partnership, or are there others?"

"There is an orphanage, and we also have joint

interest in a spa. Well, *had*, I suppose. Oh, poor Gertrude."

A footman walked in then with a tray and set it down on the low table in front of them. Lady Belmont picked up a coffee pot and looked at him with her eyebrows raised.

"I took a guess at coffee rather than tea, but I can ask them to bring the latter if you prefer?"

"Coffee is fine."

"How do you take it?"

"A little sugar. No cream."

She poured and handed him a cup. "I am never quite awake until I have had my morning coffee."

He gave her a small smile and took a sip of the rich aromatic liquid, savoring the heat and delicious bitterness that mixed in his mouth. "Did Mrs. Fox gamble?"

"Heavens no. She enjoyed a game of cards when we got together like most ladies our age, but I have never observed her *gambling*."

"And did she attend fighting matches? Boxing or wrestling, perhaps?"

Lady Belmont set down her cup with a clatter. "You ask very interesting questions, Detective."

"Her activities could help us hone in on her killer. This is important, my lady."

"All right. She did not attend fighting matches. Gertrude had a routine that she followed strictly. Every day of the week—except Sunday, of course—involved an activity involving either her businesses or charities. She squeezed in swimming at the athletics club on top of that. She was a very busy person, but not with any activity that was questionable."

"You saw her on the day she died. What was her behavior like that day?"

Lady Belmont's eyes misted. "She was very cheerful. We had an event planned for that evening. She was to host some friends at her home. A little something we did regularly for fun."

"Tell me about this event."

She waved a hand. "Oh, it was nothing important. A group of older ladies who gather to drink and gossip."

He took another sip of his coffee before setting the cup down. "Lady Belmont, I notice that you have kept indoors here at home since the incident. May I ask why?"

She huffed out a breath. "I am grieving, young man. Gertrude and I were quite close. Since I found her body, I have not slept well. I have purposely not read the papers, nor received visitors. My niece is the only one who has been here, and she apprised me of the speculations going on. I am displeased with most of them. I want Gertrude to find peace, not be the subject of gossip and innuendo."

Bennet's heart twisted in his chest as the memory of his father's murder surfaced. He swallowed and breathed slowly to tamp down the rising emotions.

"She *will* find peace, I am sure, my lady. People have only good things to say about her," he reassured.

"That is kind of you, Detective."

He was coming to understand Mary better, and the role empathy played in solving cases. People seemed more likely to open up and talk if they thought they were heard and understood. Guilt pinched his insides at the memory of suspecting Lady Belmont at the beginning of their investigation.

"On the fateful day, did you notice anyone unusual in the club, or hanging around nearby?"

She pursed her lips as she thought, then shook her head. "I do not recall seeing anyone unusual. I trained in the archery range that day—actually just before Princess Mary did the same, I believe—and then I fancied a swim. When I went to the locker room to change, I saw Gertrude." A deep sigh expanded her small chest and her shoulders rose and fell.

"I am sorry for your loss, my lady."

"Please, do what you can to bring her killer to justice, Detective."

"I will. And I know Princess Mary will, too." Bennet finished his coffee and tucked his notebook away. "Thank you for your time, Lady Belmont."

"Have a good day, Detective."

CHAPTER FOURTEEN

*M*ary was feeling more like her old self when she went downstairs to the breakfast room. She had the feeling it would be a good and productive day. Murmurs spilled out into the hall as she approached the room but the moment she appeared in the doorway, Libby and Henry fell silent. Her sister had worry lines at the corners of her eyes and her brother-in-law's expression was stony.

"What is going on?"

Libby sighed and held out the day's paper.

Mary's body went slack when she read the headline and then the article itself.

The Princess Who Is and The Earl Who Isn't

If one had taken the time to observe our dear Princess Mary at the Countess of Lynch's soireé last night, one would have found her very busy, indeed. Her keen interest in unmasking Gertrude Fox's killer—if there was, indeed, a killer at all—did not go unnoticed, for it was all she talked about; with the matrons, the spinsters, the debutantes, and the gentlemen.

Guessing the Princess's motive would have been difficult had she not been parading a bruised chin. Could such a bruise have been obtained when the late Mrs. Gertrude Fox tried to defend herself? But the princess is a sweet soul, is she not?

The evening's entertainment for the dear, sweet soul appeared to reach its peak when the princess was seen leaving a chamber in the company of the Earl of Cannington. Unchaperoned, we might add!

She felt breathless, as though she had been hit with a punching bag all over again. "What is the meaning of this? Why would they write such awful things?"

"The press has never been kind, especially to this family," Libby said. Her expression was dark. It was true. Several years ago, the press had accused Libby of murdering her kidnapper. Unfounded and soon proven wrong, of course. Had they not learnt their lesson by now?

"This is terribly unfair!" Mary continued reading the paper despite her mind warning her not to. The writer appeared to have gotten a lot of information from Margaret Seaton. False information. "They're calling me a killer because of a bruise on my chin!"

Libby gave her a commiserating look and reached across the table to give her hand a gentle pat. "It's not so bad. It's just gossip, and it will die down once they find something new to report."

"And my reputation? What happens to my reputation?"

Bender cleared his throat, interrupting them. Mary turned a glare in his direction.

"Sir Penforth Armstrong-Leeds," he announced.

"Oh, God!"

"*Mary*!" Libby admonished.

She blushed. "I apologize. I shouldn't have blasphemed."

"No, you should not," Libby said, but her rebuke was only half-hearted. Even Libby knew that Pen's arrival would likely mean trouble.

Her heart sank even deeper when her brother walked in with a thunderous expression on his face. She turned her gaze away and sank down in her chair.

"Pen! Join us for breakfast," Libby offered, trying for lightness.

"I'm not here for breakfast, Libby." He turned to Mary. "What do you have to say about today's headlines, young lady?"

"It's not my fault. I—"

"You were seen alone with a man, Mary," he growled. "Do you know how that looks?"

"I know what it looks like, Penforth. But it isn't what it is. Bennet lied to me about being an earl and I confronted him. Unfortunately, we were seen leaving the library together during the countess's soiree."

Her brother sighed and closed his eyes for a moment, his body tense. Mary wanted to crawl under a rock and hide until all of this was over.

"Let's move this conversation to a better room," he ordered, and marched out of the morning room and into the small sitting room. "Sit," he said when she entered, "and tell me exactly what has happened, starting with how you got that bruise."

Mary did as he ordered, beginning with her trip to Drysdale's Gym. His eyes narrowed to slits as he listened to her relate the events one after the other. Henry and Libby sidled into the room while she spoke. When she finished, he did not say anything for a long time.

"When I allowed you to work with DeHavillend, I expected you to behave yourself."

"I have been behaving myself," she argued. "This is just one unfortunate event."

Pen turned to Henry. "What do you two have to say, DeHavillend? Elizabeth? She's being accused of murder and on top of that, her reputation is in question."

"We can salvage this. She is a lady detective in my organization, so no one will take the murder accusation seriously. The cause of the bruise is easily proven—I am sure Drysdale will attest to that if we ask. And as for her reputation, the rumors will die down eventually. If they don't, you can always hold a gun to Bennet Brown's head and march him to the altar."

Mary burst out laughing at that ridiculous notion, and Penforth glared at both of them.

"Are you trying to be funny, DeHavillend? It is not the right time."

Henry shrugged. "What do you want me to say? Things happen, Penforth, and as you well know from past history, we can't always control them. All we can do, is control our actions and reactions moving forward."

Her brother's shoulders slumped. "That is true, I suppose. Where is this earl? I might need to have a few words with him."

Consternation filled Mary. "You're not going to force him to marry me, are you?"

Penforth turned to her, a reluctant smile appearing on his stern face. "And give you the satisfaction of sabotaging it?" He waggled a finger at her. "I will not provide you with that opportunity, my dear."

Her eyes widened, as his expression softened. "I will never force you to marry anyone you don't want. But I will still need a word with the man."

It seemed that her brother had matured. Four years ago, he'd hardly understood her at all, and their relationship had been tenuous, at best. Now, although he was still stern and prone to moods, he allowed her liberties she never thought he would have done in the past.

Perhaps it was testament to his wife Anna's positive influence on his life.

"Pen," she said in a small voice. "I am sorry. You're right. I should have been more careful."

"We will find a way to take care of this. This is not the first scandal our family have weathered."

"Certainly not," Libby muttered.

"Penforth!" Anna scolded, appearing in the doorway. "You left without me!"

His cheeks colored slightly and all the hard lines disappeared from his face. Yes, her mighty, ill-tempered brother certainly had a weakness. His wife.

Mary smirked. "Someone is in trouble," she half-mumbled.

"Be quiet!" he snapped. "I was in a hurry," he said to Anna.

"So, what is happening?"

"Pen is marrying Mary off to the earl," Libby teased, and Anna's expression turned horrified.

"Surely, you don't mean that?"

"It's true," Pen said, moving over to stand beside her.

Mary sucked in her lips and watched the scene unfold with amusement. What had started out horribly was gaining some positive color.

"And Mary is not protesting?" Anna's bright blue eyes burned.

Mary shook her head. "He's giving me no choice. It's either that, or a duel."

"A duel!" Anna practically shrieked. "That's outrageous, not to mention illegal, and... and...ridiculous!"

Henry abruptly cleared his throat, almost giving them away.

Anna took hold of her husband's coat sleeve and said firmly, "You will undo this. I thought you knew better."

Pen laughed then and the relief on Anna's face was palpable.

He took her hand in his. "Shame on you, Anna. Having so little faith in me. Do you think I can force Mary to marry? The girl is like lightning, she'd strike at all of us before we know what's happening."

"You got me for a moment." Anna laughed. "Sorry."

"We'll weather this as a family. Scandal always dies at some point."

"Thank you for understanding, Pen," Mary said, a lump suddenly forming in her throat. Her family really were rather wonderful.

"Always." He dragged her into a hug. "Anna and I will explain things to Mother," he added, pulling away. "Please, Mary, be careful."

"I will." When Anna and Pen left, she turned to Libby and Henry. "That went all right."

"Better than I thought, I'll admit," Henry said. "I think it would be best if you stayed home today. Bennet will already have met with Lady Belmont, and I will handle anything else that arises."

She nodded, agreeing with him. "I'll be upstairs in my room."

The ache caused by the many emotions inside

her returned as she began to climb the main stairs. This was as much her own fault as Bennet's. Though, if he hadn't lied to her, she wouldn't have had to pull him into that room. Now she'd been placed in an unfortunate situation, and because she was a woman, the price she'd likely pay would be heavy.

A knock on the front door arrested her progress upstairs, and she turned to see Bender admitting Lillian.

"Mary, are you all right?" Her friend hiked up her heavy skirts and rushed to meet Mary on the stairs, pulling her into a hug.

"I'll be fine, thank you."

"The press are vultures! They have no hearts."

"Let's go to my sitting room."

"What are you going to do about this?" Lillian asked when they reached the small sitting room off Mary's bed chamber.

Mary flopped onto the settee. "Let it die down. What else can I do?"

"I suppose you're right."

"Do you want to go cycling to get your mind off everything?"

"I don't wish to be seen after what has been said about me. The Lord only knows what other lies they might come up with. I'll ensconce myself here until the coast is a little clearer."

"That sounds like imprisonment, you poor thing."

Mary closed her eyes. "This is the earl's fault. If

he hadn't lied to me, I wouldn't have been seen alone with him."

"You *were* alone with him?" Lillian's eyes were wide with curiosity.

"Yes. Bennet never told me that he was the Earl of Cannington. I was furious when I found out and went to confront him."

"*Bennet Brown* is an earl?"

"Apparently. I had to find out from Lady Westwood."

"Wait!" Lillian sat upright on the other settee.

"What is it?"

"I've heard of Lord Cannington but I didn't know he was Bennet Brown. The Countess of Lynch is his cousin once removed."

Mary slowly sat up straight. "That's why he attended the event."

"Yes. Some call him the reclusive earl. But what's most fascinating about him is the fact that the late earl —Bennet Brown's father, I suppose—was murdered many years ago."

An uncontrolled gasp escaped Mary. "Oh, that's terrible! How?"

"I don't know. It was thirteen or fourteen years ago…I'm not sure. Bennet must have been in his early teens when it happened."

She suddenly felt an immense sadness on his behalf. She was still upset, but she'd just learned a little about his past.

"Poor Bennet," she whispered.

"Yes," Lillian sighed. "Life can be tough sometimes, even when you're an earl."

"How did you know about his father?"

Lillian scrunched her brows, thinking. "I probably heard Mama and one of her friends talking, I think. I remember it was some time ago."

Mary leaned back against the cushions, an exhausted sigh on her lips.

"I should go now, Mary. We have church later. Will you be all right?"

"Yes, Lilly, I'll be all right."

Her friend gave her a hug before leaving.

CHAPTER FIFTEEN

*T*wo hours later, Mary was restless and stressed. She couldn't remain indoors any longer. She'd go insane. She put on her jacket and hat and asked for her bicycle to be brought out, but not to the front of the house.

Instead, she snuck out through the servants' entrance located at the side of the house. She rode aimlessly for a while, careful not to linger anywhere she might be known, before eventually making her way to the Boston Athletics Club for Women. It was closed, but as a detective on the case, she had been given a key.

Some target practice on the archery range should help relieve the stress that was threatening to undo her wellbeing. She could also check the locker room again for more evidence. There was a slim chance that Gertrude's murderer had returned to the scene yet again.

It turned out she didn't need the key. The door was once again unlocked. Was Martha being sloppy, or had someone picked the lock?

Once inside, Mary had to blink several times for her eyes to adjust to the dark interior. Her boots against the wooden floor echoed through the narrow hallway, alerting her to how alone in the building she was.

She collected a bow and a quiver of arrows from the archery storage room, then passed back through the building on her way to the range. When she reached the front room where Cecil's desk was located, she realized that she might not be alone in the building after all. Papers were strewn all over the normally tidy desk. Her heart began to beat faster.

On her tiptoes and with her breath held, Mary crept through the building to the locker rooms where she suspected she might find activity.

The sight of many lockers broken—some with the doors completely removed and some hanging on one hinge—had her hand coming up to cover her mouth. The room had thoroughly been searched. Slinging her bow across her body together with the quiver, she decided to do a quick search for clues before calling Henry or Bennet.

The intruder was either trying to cover up their tracks, or looking for something. Their next victim, perhaps? From what she could deduce, they were likely looking for something, or someone. When one covered their tracks, they did not tend to make even more of a mess.

She headed toward Martha's office and paused outside the closed door. She should telephone Henry at once. But she also wanted to ascertain the extent of the damage. So, she continued down the hall to the swimming chamber, checking rooms as she went. She was not particularly nervous because it looked as if the intruder or intruders had left. But she was still cautious.

The swimming room was empty, though someone had been in there, too. The white tiled floor bore muddy footprints. Mary squatted down and studied them. Too large and wide to be female. She traced the path the footprints made but it did not lead her anywhere except around in circles.

She made her way back down the hall to Martha's office. The criminals were good with locks. They wouldn't have searched this building without looking in the manager's office. Then her heart thudded right up into her mouth with shock.

The door was open, and it had been shut when she passed it only a few minutes ago.

Mumbling voices filtered into the hall, freezing Mary in place.

BENNET CURSED UNDER HIS BREATH WHEN HE READ the contents of the newspaper. This was all his fault.

Mary would never have been compromised like this if he had simply told her the truth from the beginning. The suggestion that Gertrude Fox had tried to defend herself from Mary and given her a bruise would not hold—it was too utterly ridiculous—so he was not overly concerned about that part of the scurrilous article.

It was the matter of her reputation that concerned him the most. She was a lovely lady who did not deserve to have a stain on her reputation, no matter how small. It was one thing to raise eyebrows as an emancipated woman who wanted a career as well as a place in society. It was quite another to have her reputation besmirched with sly innuendo.

He had to help her repair this, somehow. Even if it meant marrying her. He opened his door to leave for her house and almost ran into a tall, dark-haired man blocking the entrance. He had an air of command about him that Bennet instantly found suffocating.

The man did not need to introduce himself, for Bennet already knew who he was. He quietly stepped away from the door and waved Mary's brother inside.

"Have you read the paper?" Sir Penforth Armstrong-Leeds asked.

"Yes, sir," Bennet replied. "I am terribly sorry for what has happened and I am willing to do whatever it takes to make amends."

Sir Penforth turned his dark eyes on him. "If I asked you to marry my sister, would you do it?"

"Yes, I would."

"Good. But I am not going to ask that of you. Unless Mary wishes it."

Bennet knew he was probably the last man Mary would want to marry. Not after breaching her trust. "I understand."

"I wanted to gauge your character. Find out if you were willing. I would hate to hold a gun to your head and march you to the altar." His lips curved up slightly, and Bennet blinked several times in bewilderment.

Sir Penforth was known for his brooding demeanor. Watching him enjoy a private joke was faintly unsettling.

"If Mary wishes it, I will marry her. I hold your sister in the greatest esteem."

As he spoke, he realized his feelings for Mary went beyond esteem, to something else altogether.

Penforth studied him a moment longer, and then nodded as if satisfied. "My business here appears to be concluded," he said. "And I do not wish to keep you from wherever you were about to rush off to. Good day, Lord Cannington."

Bennet gave him a nod as he left. "Good day, sir."

For the first time, he did not mind being called by his title. Since his father's death, he had flinched every time someone called him Cannington instead of Bennet Brown.

He still remembered how his father's death had been announced to him.

He'd just returned home from an outing with his friends one summer, happy to be reunited with them after being away at boarding school. When their usually cheerful butler, Seymour, opened the door, his eyes were grim and his face shadowed. The house he'd grown up in did not feel like home. A dark shadow had taken over; the shadow of death.

Sobs from the drawing room clenched his insides and twisted. His body began to tremble. Quinn, his father's assistant, stepped out of the drawing room and came to stand in front of him. They were about the same height even though Bennet was only just turned fourteen years old.

Quinn placed his hand on Bennet's shoulder and said, "You are the Earl of Cannington now, Bennet. You will need to be strong, Lord Cannington."

Bennet had reeled backward and was caught by Seymour as a sound that was less human and more animal reverberated out of his chest, anger and grief warring.

Bennet shook the memory away and walked out of his apartment. He'd never forgiven Quinn for breaking the news to him like that. But there was no time to dwell on the past today. He had a case to solve and he needed to win back the good favor of a woman he was especially fond of.

He called his carriage and drove to the DeHavillend residence, but was informed in the foyer that Mary was not in.

"Do you know where she is?"

Bender said, "No, my lord."

"Did she go on foot?" Her means of conveyance might give him an idea of where she'd gone.

"She rode her bicycle."

"Thank you, Bender. Is the Viscount in?"

"Yes, I am."

He looked up to see DeHavillend coming down the stairs.

"I'm sorry. It's my fault that Mary is in the papers."

DeHavillend waved a hand. "Mary is used to being in the papers."

"But it's different this time. This is a scandal."

"Well, it was not in anyone's control…only the journalists who published that nonsense. It will die down, eventually."

"I wanted to speak with her but I understand she's not at home."

"I wanted to speak with her, too." He sighed like a beleaguered man. "I advised her to remain at home but Mary hardly ever does what she is told."

"Sir Penforth paid me a visit this morning."

"Ah. And how did that go?" He held up a hand. "Before we continue, I have arranged for us to meet Gertrude's lawyers at Allebie and Anderson Law Firm. That's why I was looking for Mary. It was her idea, and I thought she would like to attend. But no matter. We can leave shortly."

"You arranged it this quickly? And on a Saturday?"

"I *am* Detective DeHavillend," he joked. "Now, back to your morning caller."

"He came to ask if I am willing to marry Mary should the occasion arise. I agreed."

DeHavillend smirked. "Did he threaten you?"

"No, he was very calm and understanding. I believe he even made a joke. Something about a gun to the head, and an altar?"

DeHavillend chuckled and clapped him on the shoulder, steering him out the door. "Then consider yourself fortunate. My brother-in-law must have approved of you, to make a joke like that. And Penforth's approval is quite a difficult thing to obtain."

"I gathered."

DeHavillend returned to the case. "The sketch artist will be at the office by the time we return." He pulled out a gold watch from his waistcoat pocket and checked it. "And the posters of both male suspects should be ready by the evening."

Bennet found himself smiling at the detective's efficiency. It was as inspiring as it was intimidating. He had clearly made the right choice, having DeHavillend mentor him, and that gladdened him more than anything.

"Excellent." Bennet climbed into his carriage and DeHavillend quickly followed.

In less than a half hour, the two men were in front

of the building that housed the Allebie and Anderson Law Firm. A man who looked to be in his forties walked up to them and DeHavillend introduced him as Ian Allebie, one of the partners of the firm.

"A pleasure to meet you, Detective Brown. Please come with me." He led them into his office.

"We have prepared the records you requested. All of Mrs. Fox's transactions since we took over the management of her finances are here." He pushed several folders toward them.

"How long have you been managing Mrs. Fox's finances?" Bennet asked.

"Seven years, Detective," Mr. Allebie replied. "We did not initially offer financial management services and Mrs. Fox was one of our first clients."

"That is quite a long time," he observed, opening one of the folders and looking through the transactions for payment made to or received from unknown organizations.

Mr. Allebie chuckled. "We pride ourselves on our ability to retain our clients."

"Hmm." Bennet was not paying attention, and neither was DeHavillend.

Nothing out of the ordinary was found in the first folder, nor the second or third, but the fifth had something. An unusually large sum had been taken out from her bank account, and the field where the name of the recipient was supposed to be was blank.

"Look at this." He showed DeHavillend.

"What can you tell us about this transaction, Mr. Allebie?" DeHavillend asked.

"Ah, yes. There was an incident two years ago, when a co-signatory removed that sum from the account without her knowledge. A covert investigation was carried out by us, as Mrs. Fox did not want the matter to be made public. She disliked scandals."

"Who was the co-signatory?" Bennet asked.

Mr. Allebie's face stiffened slightly before he answered. "Her brother, Charles Whittaker."

The two detectives looked at each other before turning to the lawyer. "Did she take any action against him?"

"No legal action was taken, but he became heavily indebted because we were unable to trace or recover any of the funds."

Charles Whittaker could have a motive to murder Gertrude. "Does he stand to inherit anything now that she is deceased?" Bennet asked.

"They have a shared property in Edinburgh, Scotland. He inherits the entire property upon her death."

Bennet looked to DeHavillend and they shared a knowing look. "We have the information we require. Thank you for your assistance, Mr. Allebie."

Mr. Allebie held out his hand to them both. "If you need anything else, please do not hesitate to contact us."

"What do you think?" DeHavillend asked after they'd stepped out of the building.

"It's a motive. He took money from her in the past. The chance to gain full control of a property might be enough to entice someone to kill."

"Let's return to the office and go over the entire case. I will send word for Mary to join us there."

CHAPTER SIXTEEN

Mary sucked in her breath and held it, torn between backing away and listening hard. She chose the latter, at least for several seconds.

"You fool!" announced one voice. "If we make another mistake, the boss will have our heads!" The man's voice was raspy.

"I'm looking, I'm looking! No need to bite my ear off," said the other man. His voice was weaker, but still menacing.

They rattled something that sounded like a drawer being pulled out.

"There's nothing here. I swear it. I already looked in that one."

"Move, let me check."

More rattling, and then something crashed to the ground and shattered. Mary winced, guessing it was most likely the porcelain ballerina that Martha loved. She was definitely going to miss that.

"There is nothing here! Let's go."

Mary dashed across the hall and snuck as quietly as she could into the nearest room—a storeroom. For a few moments, her heartbeat was the only sound in her ears. She tried to slow her breathing and calm herself. The two men's voices rose as they moved closer, and she pressed her ear to the door.

"Let's check the front desk again. Maybe we'll find the address there. We cannot fail this time. We are dead if we kill the wrong woman again. It has to be Martha Goodings, next time."

Mary's hand covered her mouth as her eyes pooled. Gertrude Fox had never been the target. The killers had made a mistake. A horrible, deadly mistake.

And now they were after Martha, on the trail of what must have been their original target.

Her trembling hand reached for the door handle and opened it a crack. She saw the retreating forms of the two men. They weren't familiar to her, but they both wore derby hats, reminding her of the description Bennet had provided about the man at the coroner's office. They vanished out of sight and she waited, listening with her heart in her throat.

After a while, laughter roared. One of them said loudly, "Here it is."

"Let's go," said the other.

Mary could not allow them to get to Martha and

kill her, too. She grabbed the bow off her shoulder and an arrow from her quiver, and bolted out of the storeroom, her bow raised. The men saw her approaching and their mouths dropped open, before they took to their feet, running toward the exit at the back of the building. She ran down the hall after them, aiming as she went. She fired and missed.

They escaped out the door. She followed, nocking her bow with another arrow. The wind was strong outside and it interfered with the next shot she fired. Still, she did not give up. She aimed again, bringing the taller of the men into focus. Her breath caught and held. She had never fired at a person before. She almost gave up, but then thought of Gertrude Fox's lifeless face staring up at her. She released the arrow and watched it's flight. The wind shifted the arrow slightly to one side but it hit the taller man in his arm. He stumbled forward before quickly regaining his footing. He rounded the corner, exiting the alleyway while clutching at his arm.

Mary felt sick at what she'd done, but she didn't have time to consider it. Instead, she continued to run after the men but they proved too fast and they were soon approaching the busier part of the street. She slowed down and eventually came to a stop, her lungs aching from the lack of air. Mary bent and heaved in huge gulps until her lungs began to return to normal. Tears of frustration and horror stung her eyes.

She straightened after catching her breath and regaining some of her composure, and ran back to the gym to call for help from the telephone in Martha's office.

"Why did I not call for help earlier?" she hissed, reprimanding herself. If she'd put aside her pride and called Bennet or Henry before now, she wouldn't be in this position, and Martha wouldn't be in such imminent danger. They'd have arrived by now and all of this would have been over before it began.

Now, the murderers were on their way to Martha's house and her futile attempts to stop them had failed.

She dialed the office and while she was waiting for the call to be connected, her eyes caught the time on the clock hanging on the wall. She sucked in a breath, then slapped her palm on the desk. "Darn it!"

What was wrong with her today? It was lunchtime, and neither of the men would be in the office at that time. She hung up and called for connection to the DeHavillend residence, rocking back on her heels restlessly as she waited for a response.

"DeHavillend Res—"

"Bender, it's Mary! Where is Henry?"

"Out, Your Highness," Bender said calmly.

"What about Bennet?"

"He was here earlier, but the gentlemen have not returned."

She let out a curse word, not caring that Bender had heard her. "When they come back, either one of them, tell them to meet me at the home of Mrs.

Martha Goodings. It is urgent. The lady's life depends upon it. The men we are after are heading there."

"Right away, Miss Mary," Bender replied with more life in his voice. He must have understood her urgency.

She dropped the handset and set her jaw. It was now up to her to go after those men.

IF THERE WAS ONE THING THAT MARY ABIDED BY IN her life, it was that she was her own champion. She did not depend on anyone else to help her, when it was a task she might be able to undertake herself.

Under ordinary circumstances, she would never chase down criminals on her own, or even ride through the streets of Boston with a bow and a quiver of arrows slung over her back, but these were not ordinary circumstances. And she had no choice. Besides, it was a cold Saturday afternoon with less people on the street, and no police officers visible on patrol to pull her up and scold her.

"Oh, Lord, please help me," she whispered as she rode. The street had grown darker with the skies becoming even more overcast and tiny cold droplets of autumn rain beginning to fall. There was a fog that was slowly rolling in, too, hampering her visibility. She pushed on, wondering if she would be able to spot the criminals even if she did catch up to them.

Her legs already ached from the force of her

pedaling, and there was a good distance between the gym and Martha Goodings' house, but she didn't care. She had wicked men to catch and bring to justice.

She did not spot them on the way. She parked her bicycle haphazardly and ran up the short steps to the front door. Instead of using the brass knocker, she pounded on the door with her fists. It was no more effective than the knocker but her patience had long run out. Her thoughts twirled as fear raced through her system.

Martha opened the door herself, looking first annoyed and then shocked. Mary pushed her back inside, slamming the door firmly shut behind them.

"Mary? Wha—"

"You are in danger from two men. No time to explain!"

Martha was dressed as if she were about to head out to a social outing. Or perhaps she had just returned?

"I don't understand."

"Is there anywhere you can hide, Martha?"

To her credit, the woman nodded and took Mary through the house to the pantry.

"Stay there," Mary ordered. "I'll check the rest of the house."

Martha's home was a narrow townhouse with three levels which would make her search relatively easy.

"I am not hiding in the pantry unless you tell me

what is going on!" Martha resisted Mary's insistent push toward the pantry and stood firm.

The words rushed out of Mary almost in a near-garbled form. "The men who killed Gertrude were at the club. I chased them and shot one with an arrow. But they said they are after you, Martha. You were the target all along, not Gertrude."

Martha's mouth dropped open, and this time when Mary shoved her in the pantry, she stayed.

"Is it lockable?" Mary asked.

"No, but I'll barricade it with something. Oh, Mary, have you called for help?"

"I left word for Bennet and Henry."

Martha slammed the pantry door shut and Mary heard her moving things around.

She started with the first floor, sweeping through the living room, small study and back to the kitchen. Then she ran up the stairs to the second floor where the bedrooms were located. Martha was a widow with no children. She quickly searched the three rooms on that level but no one else was there. Perhaps on her bicycle, she had beat the men here.

But something in her gut told her to stay on her guard and remain wary.

She raced up the next set of stairs to the top floor, which had only one room off the landing—a storage room. It was empty of people, too.

She released a relieved breath. Now to get Martha out of here and away before the men arrived. She started down from the top level when male voices reached her. Henry and Bennet? Her heart, already racing from a mixture of exertion and terror, jumped at the thought of help arriving in such a timely manner. But when she took a peek, she saw a man with lank-looking hair and a cigarette dangling from his mouth, heading into one of the bedrooms.

She froze and for a moment felt lost and uncertain of what to do. Luckily, the moment of panic disappeared, and she crept down and past the bedroom on her tiptoes. As soon as she was past, she scurried down to the next level.

The other man was there, sculking around and obviously looking for Martha. He hadn't seen her yet. His arm was roughly bandaged in white cloth that looked like bed linen torn into strips. This was the man she had shot!

They must have taken the time to stop and steal linen from somewhere. That could explain why she had arrived at the house before them. He strode across the kitchen and she ducked into the lounge area, readying her bow and loading up an arrow.

Could she do this, at such close range? Could she do it at all, knowing she might actually end up killing another human being?

A rattling noise from the kitchen convinced her. He was shaking and pushing at the pantry door, and her ears caught a faint moan of terror from Martha.

I have to do this, she thought. There's no one else.

She stepped around into the kitchen doorway, and

as the man readied to punch in the pantry door, she released her arrow.

It went straight into the man's shoulder exactly as intended. She wanted only to incapacitate him if she could. He roared in shock and pain, and crumpled to the floor. This was the second time today she'd fired at a live target and she almost dropped her bow as her mind reeled.

The work she had chosen to pursue was difficult and often dangerous, and she understood that there would be times when she would have to do unpleasant things in order to save people. But nothing had prepared her for the sense of horror that ran through her as she stared at the man bleeding on the floor.

She heard the other man's footsteps thundering as he raced down the stairs and toward her, shaking her out of her stupor.

She ran to the pantry door and turned, fumbling with an arrow that wouldn't seem to sit in place. He was too fast and too close for her to properly aim. His hand rose up and she caught the glint of a knife.

Her back hit the pantry door. Panic rose from the bottom of her stomach and her knees threatened to buckle under her. Survival instinct took over and she slid away from the door as he lunged at her.

If only she'd had more than one self-defense lesson. As she tried to regain her balance and ready for a kick, the pantry door flew open. The man hurtled into the edge of the door, falling to the floor and landing on his own weapon. He groaned and promptly lost consciousness. Martha rushed out with a rolling pin in her hands, her eyes darting around.

"Are you all right, Mary?"

Mary blinked at her, reeling from the aftermath of what had just happened. "Y-yes…I think so. Yes. I am."

No, she was not all right. But she didn't want to admit that to anyone.

Martha bent and checked the unconscious man's pulse. "He is still alive," she said. Beside him, the man Mary had shot in the shoulder was moaning weakly with pain.

A wound to his shoulder was not enough to render him unconscious, but given he'd already been wounded once today, this second time seemed to have stopped him from trying to escape.

"Are you sure you're all right, Mary?" Martha asked again, ducking into the pantry and back out with a bundle of ropes.

Mary nodded mutely.

"Then help me tie them up, dear."

Mary assisted Martha in binding the wrists and ankles of the unconscious man first, then the second. He groaned with pain when they pulled his arm forward to tie his wrists together.

"Oh, shut up!" Martha hissed. She turned to Mary once the men were securely restrained. "I believe I know why they were after me. I used to be a Pinkerton's agent in my youth. I left that life behind when I married my late husband. I never realized it might catch up with me, one day."

"That answers a lot of questions." Mary finally felt calm enough to speak, though directly after, a shuddering breath shook her. "We have them now."

"Yes, thanks to you. Mary, what you have done today is incredible."

She nodded, unsure how to answer. *I shot someone,* she wanted to say. *And it felt…awful.* She did not even know what she was feeling at this moment. She was happy, sad, drained…everything was happening to her all at once. "Do you have a telephone?" she asked. "I think we need to contact the police."

"Unfortunately, I do not but I know someone we can send with a message. Did you come here on your bicycle?"

"Yes."

"Good. I'll stay and keep an eye on these men. Go to the house two doors up on the right when you exit the front door, and ask for Jimmy. He can get a message fast enough to the police."

Mary did as suggested and found the neighboring house. A teenage boy answered her knock. He appeared to have an excess of exuberance and beamed at her.

"I'm looking for Jimmy. Martha Goodings sent me."

"Oh, that's me." He grinned.

"Can you please take a message to the police station? It's rather urgent."

"Of course. I can even run if you want me to, although it's a bit far to run all the way."

Mary held up a hand. "That won't be necessary. You can borrow my bike."

His eyes immediately began to shine with excitement. "You have a bike?"

She gave him a weary smile. "Yes, I do. Follow me."

When he saw the bike, his eyes glinted even more. "I love bikes!"

So did she, but did not tell him that. While he admired her bike, she went back into Martha's house and wrote a quick note explaining what had happened in as few words as possible, and asking them to come immediately. She signed her name as Detective Mary Armstrong-Leeds.

"Here." She gave Jimmy the note. "We have two very bad men tied up in there. Ride as you've never ridden before."

His mouth dropped open and he jumped onto the bicycle. "You can count on me." He raced off, just as a carriage careened down the street and came to a halt in front of Mary. She sighed with relief when Bennet and Henry jumped down from the carriage, their eyes wide with concern.

"Bender sent word to us at the office. Where are they?" Henry asked.

"Inside. Tied up. We caught them."

Bennet stood in front of her and placed a hand on

her shoulder as Henry rushed inside. "Well done, Mary."

Before she could say anything, he'd rushed inside after Henry. She followed more slowly, arriving at the kitchen to find them standing over Gertrude's killers.

"This is him," Bennet said in wonder, pointing at the greasy-haired criminal. "This is the man I saw at the coroner's office. And this other one has the same build as the man I chased down the alley."

"Our other theory is thrown out the window," Henry said.

"What theory?" Mary asked.

"I'll explain later," Bennet said. "Now we need to ask Mrs. Goodings a few questions."

"Let's all move to the living room, shall we?" Martha said. "I'll put on some tea."

They followed her to the living room and Mary slumped against the cushions of a sofa and closed her eyes, numbness shrouding her completely.

CHAPTER SEVENTEEN

*B*ennet knew Mary was not all right. At first, he'd thought that she was still upset with him, but after seeing the blank look in her eyes and her sluggish movements, he thought he understood. She'd chased down two criminals and shot an arrow into another human being. That must have taken something from her.

He sat down beside her on the sofa and took both of her hands in his. Her body tensed and she turned to him with visible surprise. He ran his thumbs in slow circles on the backs of her hands and she began to relax.

"I used to be a Pinkerton's agent," Mrs. Goodings began to explain. "Now that I know *I* was the real target and not poor Mrs. Fox, I am not surprised by this attack. I was involved in a lot of strike-breaking in the past. Right before my retirement, I began to receive threats from unions. Naturally, I ignored them.

They became more sporadic over time, and I really thought that part of my life was done." She sighed deeply. "And now this. It's really such a tragedy that Gertrude had to suffer. I deeply regret it."

"There was nothing you could have done," Bennet murmured, sending her a commiserating smile.

"Do you know the men?" DeHavillend asked, taking notes.

Mrs. Goodings shook her head slowly from side to side. "I've never seen these two. They may have been hired just for this job, or perhaps they're from one of the unions. In the past, the threats were always in written form." She stood. "I'll check on that tea now."

Bennet returned his attention to Mary. He did not like her pallor. "How are you?" he whispered.

She opened her eyes but did not answer him immediately. "I don't know, Bennet."

He gave both of her hands a gentle squeeze. "It's going to be all right. I'll stay with you until you feel better."

Mrs. Goodings returned and poured everyone a cup of tea. When she offered Mary a cup, the princess declined with a slight shake of her head. Bennet moved closer to her on the sofa.

"We will have to further investigate this case," DeHavillend declared. "Catching these killers does not close it. If someone sent them after you, they could send more. We need to know who is behind it."

"Thank you, Detective."

The boy Mary had sent to fetch the police returned then, red-faced and out of breath. "They're…" The boy paused to breathe. "They're here."

"Thank you, Jimmy," Mrs. Goodings said.

Everyone crowded into the kitchen then, with the police captain and two patrolmen who had arrived to apprehend the criminals.

JIMMY SLUMPED AGAINST THE COUNTER, OBVIOUSLY tired from his frantic bicycle ride. Mary knew how he felt. Every bone in her body ached with exhaustion. To her surprise, Bennet fetched the boy a glass of water, clapping him on the back. "Good work, young man."

"Thank you, Detective." Jimmy raised the glass gratefully to his lips.

This was another side of Bennet that she was seeing. He was usually a little brusquer, but to see him care for the boy with that small touch of kindness, made her feel better toward him. And his gesture of support when he'd held her hand moved her. She didn't think Henry had noticed anything amiss with her.

"What is your name?" Bennet asked him.

"Jimmy, sir."

Bennet nodded approvingly before joining Henry.

The rest of the happenings in Martha's house

became a blur, and when everything was finally sorted and they were allowed to leave, Bennet helped her into Henry's large carriage and seated himself beside her. Henry sat opposite them. The ride passed in silence with her hand in Bennet's warm, comforting ones. Now and then, he would give it a small squeeze. She found herself leaning in to him and gaining comfort from the connection.

She wanted to thank him for his support but words for some reason seemed to be beyond her. The ordeal had shaken her more than she expected.

They arrived home and all Mary wanted to do was crawl into bed and sleep away the dreariness from her mind. She left them and dragged herself across the hall to the foot of the stairs.

"Mary," Libby called, stepping out of the drawing room with a gurgling Amelia in her arms. "Bender told us you called. Have you solved the case?"

"Yes," she muttered and climbed a step.

"Here." Libby thrust the baby into her arms. "Holding Amelia might do you some good."

"Libby," she began to protest. "I really don't think now is a good idea for me to…" The baby's weight settled in her arms and her cute little face, smiling up at Mary, made her change her mind. She held Amelia closer and began to rock her, enjoying the warmth and the fresh, innocent baby smell.

"See? I told you that you need it. Babies relieve stress sometimes."

Mary tried to scoff, but it was weak. "I thought they created the stress."

"*When* they are peaceful, they relieve stress." Libby gently took her arm and began to steer her toward the drawing room. "Come, Anna and the children are here."

Mary resisted, unsure. "Libby…I don't…" she sighed. "I don't think I want to see anyone else right now. It's been an odd sort of day. I…err…I shot someone with my bow and arrow."

Libby's brows drew with worry. "Oh, my goodness! Mary, I didn't realize how much strain you'd been through. Shall we go upstairs, then?"

The pitter-patter of tiny feet stopped them and the owners of those tiny feet ran up and clutched Mary's skirt.

"Aunt Mawy!" the children shouted in unison.

"Aunt Mawy!" Little Rose looked up at her, her bright blue eyes sparkling. "Can you wead uth a thtowy?"

"Oh, Rose…"

"Pleath!" she begged, her lisp warming Mary's heart.

"Yes, Aunt Mawy!" Jeremy echoed, pulling at her skirt.

"How could one say no to those adorable little faces?" came Bennet's voice. He picked Jeremy up and tossed him in the air. The boy squealed with delight.

Mary discovered she was smiling. The numbness

that had overtaken her was wearing off. She did not need to be alone to return to her senses. She only needed to be surrounded by the people she cared about most in this world.

Jeremy on his shoulder, Bennet took Rose's hand and pulled her away from Mary. "Let's go and pick out a fun story to read, shall we?"

"I love thtowies!" Rose toddled with Bennet into the library.

"Feeling better?" Libby asked.

Mary nodded, turning to see Anna in the drawing room doorway. She waved and smiled. Mary would give them the details of the case later.

"Do you have a moment, Mary?" Henry appeared in the hall.

"Yes." She handed Amelia back to Libby and followed him into his study.

"I am happy to see that you are looking more like yourself." He poured sherry into two glasses and handed her one. Raising it in a toast, he said, "To your success today and to many more in the future."

She raised her glass before bringing it to her lips for a sip. It was only now that her triumph was starting to register.

"I am very proud of you, Mary." Henry's eyes reflected his words and a lump formed in her throat. "You were forced to act alone and you did what you had to, to save Martha Goodings. Well done."

This day had been long coming.

"Will you acknowledge me officially as Detective Mary Armstrong-Leeds?"

Henry let out a low chuckle. "Yes, Sherlock."

Finally, she was able to laugh.

That evening

BENNET STAYED FOR DINNER, AND AFTERWARD, HE AND Mary retreated to the library, careful to leave the door ajar. He told her of their theory after their meeting with the law firm that managed Gertrude Fox's finances, and she laughed and teased him about how off course he'd been.

"Oh, it's not just me. DeHavillend thought the same."

"If I'd been there, I would have assumed exactly the same," she admitted. "It is a plausible explanation. Not the correct one, as it turns out, but still…"

They lapsed into a comfortable silence, and she hoped he was taking as much pleasure in her company as she was in his. By the look in his eyes and the slight grin that lifted his lips, she suspected he was.

Eventually, she leaned forward in her chair, her dark eyes somber.

"Bennet…" She hesitated.

"Whatever it is, say it."

Her eyes met his. "It's about your father."

His jaw tightened and his body tensed for a

moment. But then he relaxed back in his chair. "Yes. It's time for me to be completely honest with you. I owe you that, Mary."

"You don't have to, but…"

"I do. And I *want* to share this with you."

Mary nodded. "I learned that your father was murdered," she prompted, trying to be gentle in her approach.

Bennet released a long sigh. "He was found dead at his club, and the investigation at the time proved fruitless. His murderer was never identified or caught."

Her hand found his. He looked deep into her eyes, searching. She hoped he would see no pity there, but merely commiseration and understanding. Bennet clutched her hand, as if drawing comfort from her touch.

"My mother was so shaken by the ordeal she slipped into melancholy. In the end, she couldn't stand the sight of me. I suppose I reminded her of what she had lost. I was the earl, and yet in her view, I wasn't. To this day she still cannot bear to see me."

"Oh, Bennet." Her heart squeezed tight at the thought of going through life without the support of her family. "I cannot imagine how tough it must have been for you."

"I have not seen her in over a year. She will not see me, but I still send her flowers every week. Her housekeeper told me once that she doesn't hate them, so that's something, I guess."

Mary's eyes widened a fraction, showing her surprise. "That is very good of you. And I'm so very glad you told me."

"No more secrets between us. I learned a tough lesson."

A small giggle emanated from her. "I forgive you."

"So, will you allow me to train you?"

"*Train* me?"

"Boxing, remember?"

"Oh!" She scowled. "Do you know, I missed my lesson at Drysdale's today."

"Then perhaps it's not meant to be. Do let me train you."

She arched her brows up. "Not meant to be? Is that your best argument, Detective?"

Bennet gave a shrug. "I am running out of ideas, Mary."

"Fine." She feigned haughtiness. "Her Royal Highness shall deign to allow his lordship to train her."

A huge smile split his face. "Excellent." He rose and held out his hand to her. "Shall we begin on Monday?" He pulled her to her feet, too.

"Certainly, Detective."

"I'll see you then." He kissed her fingers. "Good night, Mary."

"Good night, Bennet." Her voice was a barely audible whisper as she added, "And thank you, for being there today. For…noticing…and caring…"

Ever so tenderly, his fingertips caressed her cheek.

Her eyes fluttered shut at the sensation. She wished he would linger, but it was late and they were both feeling raw with the emotions of the past few days.

"Good night, my dear," he said again, before turning and walking away.

November 25, 1895

MARY DRESSED EAGERLY IN HER PROFESSIONAL-looking outfit: a thick skirt that accentuated her tiny waist, a shirtwaist, and a matching jacket. She placed her hat atop her voluminous hair and smiled confidently into the mirror.

"Bender, can you have my bike brought out to the front?" She flittered down the stairs. The smile pushing her cheeks up was unrestrained.

"Yes, Miss Mary."

"Morning, Mary." Bennet bowed.

"Bennet? What are you doing here this early?"

"Detective DeHavillend has given us leave to train before we meet him at the office. We have about two hours at our disposal."

Every muscle in her body was tender, but a promise was a promise. She had agreed to begin training with Bennet today.

"I'm riding as well," he announced as they stepped out the door.

She spotted his bicycle and grinned. "You don't ride often, do you?"

"No, I don't, but I think I will more often now."

They climbed onto their bikes and rode together to the Investigation Offices side by side. Mary took a minute to appreciate the place even more. One day, she intended to have her own detective agency where she could solve cases independently and even train other young women to become detectives like herself. It was a dream she fully intended to make a reality one day. As long and she remained spirited and steadfast, and kept her mind open to always learning new things.

The basement housed a large sparring room and gym along with an armory, which was currently locked. Provision of a practice range for both archery and shooting had been made.

It was altogether a very impressive set-up.

"Welcome to the sparring room." Bennet opened his arms in an expansive gesture. "This is the most used space in the gym, and by far my favorite area."

"I'm sure it is." She eyed several punching bags hanging from a beam on the ceiling.

"Would you like to give them a try?"

She hesitated.

"Oh, don't tell me you're afraid of a punching bag," he teased good-naturedly.

"I think I want a bigger challenge than a punching bag."

"Am *I* challenge enough?" One side of his mouth curved.

"We'll see."

"Those are weights for strength exercises." He waved in the direction of the weights. We need to match you up with the correct weight, and build up as you become stronger. Two men were already seated on benches, each lifting a weight with one arm.

"It's impressive, Bennet," she admitted.

"Yet you skipped this and went all the way across town to Drysdale's."

Mary punched his arm playfully. "I'm never going to hear the end of that, am I?"

"Probably not." He laughed and dodged her next attack, then sobered up and cast her a thoughtful look. "Before we start, would you like me to call one of the female administrative staff down, to act as chaperone? This is far more risqué than a few minutes in the countess's library, and look what happened there."

Mary bit her lip, considering. "This is a private building, so the only people who might see us are those who already work here. Technically we are not alone. Those men are here lifting their weights." She pointed to the weights area. "And you know what? I am done with worrying about what society matrons and gossipmongers might think. Let's get on with the training, Bennet."

"Are you ready?" he asked her.

"Oh, yes."

He first showed her some stretching exercises.

"I didn't know these were important." Mary raised her arms over her head, trying to copy his movements as he bent to his left, then right, stretching his lean body.

For the next training session, she would have to leave off her corset to get proper movement in her body, though she wouldn't tell Bennet that, of course.

"It loosens the muscles and prevents certain injuries. Especially muscle and connective tissue injuries."

They finished the stretches and he began to demonstrate some boxing stances and moves. Some were new, and others were the exact ones Mr. Drysdale had shown her.

"Let's spar," she suggested excitedly, eager to try out her new moves on him, but Bennet shook his head.

"You're not ready yet, Mary."

"I can handle it," she insisted, hopping from one foot to the other as she punched the air.

"We will spar when you are better trained." He sounded quite serious.

"Oh, don't spoil the good moment by being stern." She demonstrated a right upper cut near his face, just as Mr. Drysdale had shown her. He did not so much as flinch. "See? I can do it." She did it again, only this time, she caught him right on the nose. His head snapped back.

Mary's hands clapped over her mouth. "Oh, my goodness!"

Bennet was bleeding from his nose.

"Oh, Bennet, I apologize. I didn't mean to do that!" She winced from the guilt clamping over her. She reached for him, cradling his injured face in her hands.

A low chuckle was followed by a gentle shake of his head. "You can be very attentive when you're feeling guilty."

"It doesn't look too bad," she concluded, after checking his nose. "The bleeding has already slowed."

"Nothing is broken."

"I am still sorry."

She released him, and he disappeared to the far side of the room to clean off the blood with a towel and some water before returning.

"Please don't declare the training over." She chewed on her bottom lip.

Bennet's laughter rumbled from his chest. "Don't be silly. I'm going to grant your wish and we're going to spar." His eyes darkened.

Before she could prepare, he wrapped his arm around her waist and hooked one of his legs around hers. She fell backward onto the mat, the wind knocked out of her. He landed on top of her but not with his whole weight.

"Now, I understand how you got hit on the chin by a punching bag. You are very easy to distract, my dear."

She tilted her head back to look at him, more distracted than before. Her hands came up to sift through his silky dark hair, watching his lips part and his eyes flare. Her breath caught when he lowered his head and pressed his lips to hers in a soft, chaste kiss.

Oh, but she wanted more. So much more.

His grin was wide and his eyes deliciously seductive when he pushed himself up to his feet. He extended a hand and helped her up, before pressing his lips to her knuckles.

"Would you accompany me next week to the theater?" he asked suddenly. "Not for work. Just… because. I would really like that, Mary."

A squiggle of excitement tied her stomach into sudden knots. Her relationship with Bennet was fast becoming something more than what it had been. There was no label she could place on it, yet, but when she was with him, he made her feel more alive, and more *seen*, than she had ever felt before.

She couldn't believe they had only known each other a few days.

Standing on the sparring mat, staring up at his handsome face and reading the desire he no longer tried to hide, she knew that this could be the beginning of something special.

Her sister Libby, and Anna, and even their lovely friend Sarah, were truly happy with the men in their lives. And watching them over the past few years, Mary had learned from them. If you found a man who made you feel special, then you did not let him slip through your fingers.

"Yes," she answered without any indecision whatsoever. "I would love to accompany you to the theater next week, Bennet."

The End...for now

Please keep an eye out for the next instalment in the *Boston Heiresses* series, *Not Quite a Detective*, in which Mary and Bennet's story will continue.

If you would like to see where it all began, read Anna and Pen's story in

Not Quite a Duchess.

Read Libby and Henry's story in

Not Quite a Baroness.

Then read on for Sarah and the Raven's story in

Not Quite a Lady.